D1795325

MR. RED

TS LAYNE

Copyright © 2019 by TS Layne
Paperback Edition ISBN-13: 978-1-948526-11-1
EPUB Edition ISBN-13: 978-1-948526-10-4
Cover Art by Melissa Gill Designs
Published by Shady Layne Media

All rights reserved. No part of this book may be reproduced, distributed,
stored, or transmitted in any form or in any manner without written
permission except in the case of brief quotations included in critical
articles and reviews. For information, please contact the author.
This is a work of fiction. Names, characters, places, and incidents are
products of copious amounts of wine, long walks, and the author's
overactive imagination, or are used fictitiously. Any resemblance to
actual events, locales, organizations, or persons, living or dead, is
entirely coincidental.

They say redemption comes from unexpected places...

But when you've been an asshole your entire life, there's only punishment for the things you've done. So when Alison comes sweeping into my life half-dressed, wielding a frying pan, and threatening to brain me, begging for mercy is the last thing on my mind.

I never knew how much a dirty, filthy mouth pushed my buttons until her sweet lips touched my body. Until her sexy curves drove me wild with every roll of her hips. But Karma is a b*@ch, and when my reckoning comes, I could lose everything- including the woman I can't live without.

Sign up for my newsletter at www.tslayne.com to receive updates, sneak- peeks, and freebies!

Chapter One

Nico

"*I*'m sorry man, it looks like you're broke." My accountant, Brett drops his gaze, and picks at an invisible speck of dust on his desk. "Dead broke."

It takes a minute for the words to sink in before my head explodes. "What the fuck do you mean I'm *dead broke?*" All the blood has rushed up to my head, leaving my fingers and my feet numb. I flex both just to make sure I'm not having an out of body experience.

"I mean, before you signed the divorce papers, it looks like Veronica emptied every single one of your joint accounts."

I slam both my hands on the desk and lean forward. Brett flinches, but at least has the balls to meet my angry glare. "Then you better start figuring out a way to get it the fuck back," I growl, trying my best to keep my field of vision clear. "You're an accountant for chrissake."

"Who you pay to do your taxes, not babysit your millions," he snaps irritably.

I think back to dinner, to the stilted conversation between me and Brett and his wife, Maggie - the glances I caught them exchanging, the thinly veiled hints from Maggie that I've overstayed my welcome... a sick feeling comes over me. "How long have you known?"

The guilty grimace he makes gives it all away.

"How long have you known?" I repeat, anger simmering.

"Ah... ah... just a few days," he says quietly, face turning a ruddy shade of pink. "I-I wanted to be sure before I... just in case..." his voice trails off.

"Just in case *what?*" I grit, the picture becoming clearer with each moment that passes. "Just in case you could eke out a little bit more blood from the turnip? Just in case you could line your pockets just a little bit longer?" God how could I have been so naive? "Fuck, Brett, we were college roommates." But not friends. Clearly, not friends. Stupid me.

"It's not like that," he sputters.

"Oh? Then tell me, how is it?" I'm so sick of this. Of the fake friends, of the betrayal, of nothing seeming like it is. A dark voice sounds in my head. *Karma, Nico. Karma.* It's right, the voice. My house of cards has been slowly tumbling to the ground, starting with dad locking me and my brothers out of our trust fund, then Veronica kicking me out, and ultimately getting knocked up by Senator Fucking Whelan, Hollywood producer-turned-politician, then demanding a quickie divorce. I push down a cynical laugh. Ironic, that when money's involved, a five-year marriage takes only days to dissolve. And now this. She's well and truly screwed me. Hit me where I was most vulnerable. *Just like you did to Jason,* the voice points out.

Times ten. Fucking karma, indeed. "Why the fuck have I been paying you, Brett? You were supposed to look out for shit like this."

His face is the color of a beet now. "I know, I know, it's just-"

"That you were more interested in taking my money than *actually working.*" I point out, seeing the situation clearly now, for the first time. "So all that talk about friendship, about your house being my house, about how we go way back- it was all bullshit wasn't it?"

His mouth opens then shuts.

I slam my hands on the desk and rise. "*Wasn't it?*" For once, I want one of these money-grubbing assholes to just fucking be honest with their motives.

Brett opens his hands. "I'm sorry, man. I really am."

Sure he is. I shake my head and push off from the desk, mind already spinning options for what's next like a Rolodex. "Tell Maggie I said thanks for the hospitality."

"Do you have another place lined up?" The fact that he doesn't even bother to disguise the eagerness in his voice, is like a nail in the coffin to our 'friendship'.

"Yeah, yeah." Like I would tell him otherwise, or worse, beg. I pause at the door, hand on the jam. "And Brett?"

"Yeah?"

"You're fired." I head down the hall, past the man cave, where I've been sleeping on the couch for the past seven weeks, past Maggie hiding in the kitchen, to the front hall where my backpack and leather jacket hang in the corner. I haven't worn the thing since college because Veronica hated it. So when she unceremoniously kicked me out, I took perverse pleasure in grabbing it from the closet, wheeling my Ducati out of the garage, and kicking up a rooster tail of gravel as I sped off.

There's no need for a dramatic exit here. I'm done, and I just want to move the fuck on. The cool salty dew of the marine layer hits my face as I slip out the front door. Fitting, that it never cleared today. There won't be a riding off into the sunset moment for me, only disappearing into the fog. Also fitting.

I take one last look around the fancy Carmel Highlands neighborhood, with its gracious houses tucked between redwoods and rocky crags, overlooking the bay like tiny fiefdoms surveying their land. The whole reason Brett and his family live here is because of *me*. Gall burns the back of my throat. And how many others in the neighborhood are just like him? Siphoning money from the uber-wealthy to line their pockets, all in the name of *business?* The whole thing disgusts me. But what disgusts me more, is the unwitting role I played in all of it. Foolishly believing that my wealth secured loyalty, *friendship* to those I bestowed it upon.

I quickly check my phone. Weeks ago, when Veronica surprised me with divorce papers and let the tabloids inform me that she was pregnant again, this time with Senator Whelan's child, my brother Declan offered up his vineyard on Mt. Veeder. But I couldn't. At least not then. I'm the oldest of the three of us, and while it may only be by six minutes, I was the one groomed to lead, I'm the responsible one. And asking anyone for help, especially one of my brothers, would be admitting failure. But there's no use denying it anymore. I'm exactly that. Spectacularly. And it's either take my brother up on his offer, or camp on the beach.

I don't bother to text him to confirm I'm on my way. I already know it's unoccupied, except for a skeleton crew of day laborers working to rebuild the 1800's era farmhouse - I checked out the property weeks ago, just in case. I strap into my helmet and sling a leg over the bike, a part of me settling with the low purr of the engine beneath me. Tendrils of fog undulate and close in around me as I ride away - and the once billionaire prince, now fallen from his pedestal, is swallowed by the coming night.

Thanks to Friday night traffic, it's well after midnight when I roll to a stop, exhaustion pinching the space between my shoulder blades. I just fucking want to sleep. Okay, and drink. I could use a bottle of Scotch. Or bourbon. Or anything strong enough to make me pass out and forget the fucking mess I've made of my life. I cut the engine and gaze skyward. Declan scored big with this place, the air is clear and crisp, and even with the light pollution from Napa and Sonoma, and the city to the south, you can still see the stars. I didn't bother to ask him if it was planted, but you'd have to work hard to produce a shitty bottle of wine in conditions like this. The farmhouse, destroyed by fires a year ago, stands lonely and forlorn in the moonlight, lending a gothic feel to the place. To my right stands a double-wide trailer, most likely the foreman's office. Easy enough to crash there until morning when I can get my bearings.

I loop my helmet over the handlebars and hop off the bike, taking a moment to stretch before I approach the trailer. The tension across my shoulders relaxes a bit when the door quietly swings open. I flip a switch by the door and blink at the harsh overhead light. "Fancy digs," I mutter as I step into the room and drop my backpack. A desk with a laptop stands in the corner, but the rest of the space is... homey. A large leather sectional and a low modern coffee table take up most of the space. The kitchen is well equipped, and a round table with four chairs is nestled into the bay window. But what has my attention is the bottle of grappa and two small glasses at its center. It figures that Dec would have hired someone with wine knowledge. The apple doesn't fall far from the tree for any of us, even though we try.

I drop into a chair and pull over the bottle and a glass. I'd rather not drink alone- misery loves company. But beggars can't be choosers, and I need to drink away this day, this week, this summer from fucking hell. I pour a full glass and salute the empty space. "To karma," I murmur quietly, then down the contents in one swallow. The burn brings tears to my eyes, but I don't care. There will be time later to contemplate the finer points of this particular bottle, but right now, I want release. I pour another full glass and drain it.

The pleasant buzz hits after the fourth glass, and I let out a deep sigh. Exhaustion overtakes me, and I can barely lift my hand. I pour a final glass for good measure. This should allow me to sleep into next week, at least. And maybe when I wake up I'll realize it's all been some kind of a dark, twisted nightmare.

If only I was so lucky.

Chapter Two

Nico

The first thing to hit me as I regain consciousness, is the constant stabbing just above my left eye. I groan and shift, only to be hit with the second realization - that my hands and feet are bound. I blink and wince, trying to sweep the grappa induced cobwebs from my mind. I try moving my hands and feet again. Definitely bound. My heart pounds heavily against my sternum. This is a nightmare, right? My subconscious is punishing me, right? I swallow and with extreme effort, focus my eyes, suddenly aware I'm not alone. I sit up with a mind-stabbing jolt. "What in the hell? Who are you?" I croak at the scantily clad and clearly furious creature in front of me.

"Who in the hell are *you*?" she bristles, holding something head-level that takes me a minute to register as a cast-iron fry pan. "You drank my grappa," she accuses.

"So I did."

"You're trespassing."

I hold up my bound wrists, squinting, because it's too fucking bright in here. "So I am." Jesus, who in the hell is this woman? The foreman? With supreme effort I focus my eyes, and nearly choke on my own spit as the woman comes into focus. Never in my wildest dreams would I have expected to be tied up by a woman wearing some kind of big, fat rag curlers and a facial mask. The pale mask only serves to accentuate eyes so dark they're nearly black. And clearly pissed as hell. I swallow as my eyes drift lower. Scantily clad doesn't even begin to describe the sheer sleeping… thing she's wearing. So sheer, her dusky nipples and full, soft breasts call out to me like sirens. My breath catches somewhere in my chest. Her figure is lush, soft and curvy. The kind of body that begs to be squeezed and caressed. The kind of body you could lose yourself in, the kind of body that can take all of you. The polar opposite of Veronica. And God strike me dead for being a perv, but as I stare, my cock thickens, arousal pooling deep in my balls for the first time in months. Maybe even years.

"Hey. Eyes up here," she snaps.

Her voice pulls me out of my grappa-induced musings, and I make things ten times worse when I grin up at her. "Sorry, darlin'. It's not every day I'm held captive at my brother's place by a raving half-dressed lunatic in a facial mask and curlers."

She sucks in a surprised breath. "I am *not* a lunatic."

"So you do this kind of thing frequently then? Does Declan know you're here?"

"I'm calling the cops."

I lift my wrists again. "No need, sweetheart. Really. I swear I'm not going to hurt you."

"How do I know?"

"Well, for starters," I pull on the duct tape, my wrist nearly coming free. "I suggest you don't turn to a life of crime anytime soon. I could have busted out of your restraints five minutes ago."

Her eyes widen and she worries at her lower lip. "Why didn't you?"

I let out an empty laugh. "Because I'm too fucking tired, and my head hurts."

"Because you stole my grappa."

"Look, honey, if that's what's got your undies in a twist-" I drop my gaze to her hem, which is at eye level. "Are you even wearing undies?" I ask, my throat suddenly dry. She's not, and I can see the barest hint of plump pussylips flirting with the folds of her... whatever you call it. Fuck. It's the hottest thing I've seen since, ever. I shift uncomfortably, because in spite of the grappa, my cock is starving for something, anything besides my hand in the shower.

She lets out a squeak and lowers the pan, a dusky flush creeping across her chest. "I work for Declan," she grits indignantly. "But you still haven't told me who you are."

I drop my head- it takes too much effort to be upright at the moment, and I study her through half-lidded eyes. What kind of game is she playing here? She's looking at me like she knows me. *Really* knows me. But I swear I've never seen her before in my life. I don't recognize her voice, or her body. And I'm pretty sure, once the err... creative face covering is removed, I'm not going to recognize her face either. "I think you know who I am." I don't have the energy to be coy.

She lets out a sigh. "You're Nicholas Case, aren't you?"

"Nico." I raise my wrists again. "I'd shake your hand..." I shrug.

"Why are you here? Declan didn't mention anything about visitors."

The stabbing above my left eye starts again. "He

invited me here weeks ago. Ask him." I crack open an eye, immediately drawn to dark buds puckered tight and pushing through the sheer fabric, teasing me with how untouchable they are. They might as well be eyeing me through a glass wall. I force myself back to neutral territory. "So you're the foreman? Very progressive of Dec."

She makes that squeaky noise deep in her throat again. "Hardly. I'm the winemaker."

That makes me sit up, albeit too fast, as my head angrily reminds me. "Wait. Dec's making wine?" Sonofagun. He's never shown the faintest interest.

"No. *I'm* making wine. That's why he hired me. That's why-" She shakes her head. "Why'm I telling you this?"

I flash her a mischievous grin. "Because I'm the kind of guy women love to confide in." Not. *So* not. If anything, I was the kind of guy mothers forbid their daughters to date. But maybe I'm about to turn over a new leaf.

She's not buying it. She scoffs. "Good to know you're still a bullshitter," she retorts with a huff.

"Wait. *Do* we know each other?"

She freezes, but it's so fucking hard to read her with that thing covering her face, I can't tell what she's thinking. "No," she says firmly with a shake of her head. "The papers have said all anyone needs to know about you."

Truth. My brothers and I have been fodder for both the society pages and the gossip rags since we were probably sixteen. But she'd only know that if she's from here. "What did you say your name was?"

She cocks her head, eyes narrowing. "Alison."

"Alison?"

Her mouth thins as if she's having some kind of inner battle with herself. "Alison Walker."

"A pleasure to meet you. *Alison.*" I catch her eyes and let my mouth linger over her name. It's as sensuous on the tongue as her body would be underneath me. If only we could resolve the small issue of the duct tape.

Something hot flares in the deep dark depths of her eyes, and she clears her throat. "Stay here."

Like I'm going anywhere. I stare unabashedly as she turns and hurries down the hall, still clutching the frying pan. Her barely-there nighty barely covering the plump curves of her ass as it sways in time with her hips.

Holy. Hell.

Maybe there's a silver lining in this nightmare after all.

Chapter Three

Alison

Shit. Damn. Fuck.
Shit. Damn. Fuck.

*Shit*DamnFuck. The words keep repeating in my brain, faster and faster as I rush down the hall to my bedroom. I canNOT believe that Nicholas Fucking Case is duct taped on my couch. That *I* duct taped him. That he stared at me like he wanted to lick me from head to toe, like I weighed 110 not 172. He stared like he was visualizing me with no clothes on. Okay, I have no clothes on... well, barely- but I look like a freak. I'm wearing a rose-scented moisture mask and my hair is in rag rollers. I should have thought to grab a robe, but when I heard snoring loud enough to shake the windows coming from the living room, my thought wasn't about modesty, it was about fucking survival.

I'm flushed. Heated. Fluttery. And not from embarrassment, although there's plenty of that, too. I'm *aroused*. My pussy is slick with want, responding to the naked desire in Nico's eyes as he stared at me. *Me.* Not some praying mantis runway model with legs for days, but *me*. I shake my head. He must have grappa goggles. It's the only sound explanation for the way he looked at me like he wanted to fuck me- *hard*. And god help me, but I want that too. Even if Nico Case is my worst nightmare.

I peel off the mask and drop it into the trash, reaching for a washcloth. Normally my morning ritual gives me peace, helps set my frame of mind. But my skin is hyper-sensitive. My nipples are achy and dying to be pinched. And the throbbing between my legs... I squeeze my thighs together, because I can't take it. I'm strung tighter than a bowstring. I pull my fingers through my wetness and circle my clit. It's been ages since I've been this turned on, this... *hungry*. I bend over the sink, working faster, alternately pinching and circling my clit. Release comes quickly, and with it, a flood of shame. I just rubbed off a quickie because of Nico Case - instrument of torture for two years of my life, and haunting me for many years after. *Land-whale, cow, beluga.* I hang my head, hand still clutching the sink as the litany of all-too familiar names rings in my memory. The stealing of my glasses, or my textbooks. The snide remarks in class. All of it. I drag in a slow breath. The only place Nico belongs is out of my life and as far away from me as possible. I pull out the rag curlers and let my hair fall in ringlets below my shoulders. When I've set the last one aside, I catch my hair up in a scrunchy. I'll comb it out after my walk. After my phone call to Declan.

I pull on my exercise tights, self-conscious for the first time in a very long time about the way my thighs rub together, about the spread of my hips. It's the same when I yank my favorite sports bra over my head- the one that's supposed to make me feel sexy, strong and capable. Instead, all I can see is how my breasts mash together to form a uniboob, and the way the flesh on my arms wobbles when I reach my hands overhead.

I lace up my shoes, then reach for my favorite sweatshirt with the mesh side panels and zip it up halfway, so the skin below my uniboob is just visible. I stare into the mirror at what was supposed to be my new and improved self. The badass version of me who's a talented winemaker with a take no prisoners attitude, which my boss happens to love. For an awful, dark moment, I'm swallowed by self-loathing, by all the insults and aggressions that even after so many years, lurk dangerously close to the surface. The affirmations I've plastered in bright colored stickies around the edge of my mirror pull me back from the edge.

Fuck it.

I didn't work hard for all these years to let those thoughts best me.

Fuck him.

I grab my cell phone from the dresser and slip it into my side thigh pocket- one of the features I love most about this pair of exercise tights. I don't care what time it is in Kansas, I'm calling Declan as soon as I get out of the house. I hurry down the hall, trying- and failing- to avoid looking at the large expanse of sexy, hard man reclining on my couch. "Hey, where are you going?" he calls.

"Out. Make yourself at home," I add sarcastically. Although, truth be told, he could easily undo the duct tape. It's not my best work. But it was early and I was scared, and it took me a hot minute to recognize the face of my intruder. Nico's changed. Not as much as I have, but enough that I didn't recognize him at first. For starters, he grew a million inches, and he filled out. Extremely nicely, as I discovered while I was taping his wrists and ankles.

There's not an inch of fat on the man's body- just one-hundred-percent rock hard muscle from top to toe. He was always good looking in a kind of dark and twisty Heathcliff sort of way, but now his face has lost its teenage softness, leaving high cheekbones and a sharp jawline covered in sexy stubble. His mouth is still full, and for a second it distracts me as it pulls into a sardonic smile.

"Toodles," he says, waving his fingers and winking. *Fucking winking.* "Don't do anything I wouldn't do."

Heat explodes across my chest, and I turn before I say something stupid, pushing out the door and letting it slam shut behind me. Outside, I gulp the cool morning air. There's just a hint of dew on the nose, and I can't help but get a little bit excited to check the grapes this morning. Growing conditions have been perfect for ripening- long warm days, not too hot, and cool, crisp nights, with the barest hint of sea air. Not enough moisture to promote fungus or rot, just enough to keep the plants happy.

I pull out my phone as I cross the dirt expanse between the farmhouse and the outbuildings. Behind them is the best view on the property- southwest-facing vines pitched steeply, surrounded by redwoods and the encroaching forest that comprises most of Mt. Veeder. Fog has settled in the lower elevations, giving up here an almost otherworldly feeling. I can see why the Italians planted here in the 1800s. It must have reminded them of home. But I can't afford to get lost in my surroundings this morning. I have an intruder to remove. I pull out my phone and ring Declan.

It goes to voice mail.

No way. He's *not* not answering his phone. The man is a workaholic. He's up, and he's fucking taking my call. I ring again. And again, and again, and again.

"*What?!?*" he yells into the phone when he finally

answers. "This better be damned good."

Shit. He's in a mood. I probably interrupted him while he was having sex. That would be just my luck. "I'm sorry, I know it's a Saturday, but this couldn't-"

"What's going on," he barks.

I can tell I've pissed him off, and start to stammer. "Do you have a minute? Okay, even if you don't-" I take a big breath, trying to get a handle on my out of control emotions. "*Why is your brother here?*"

"You mean Nico?"

Something inside me snaps. Who the fuck else would I mean? "Unless Austin took the redeye and no longer looks like your twin," I bark back.

His voice immediately changes to concern. "Why is Nico at my vineyard? Is he bothering you?"

So Declan didn't invite him? I am going to kick his ass out of here so fast his head spins. "I have no idea, and yes."

"Yes? He's bothering you? Tell him I said to knock it the fuck off."

That will go over well. I can see it now when I tell him that. He'll look at me with those dark eyes and laugh. "Why is he here, Declan?" Jesus, I really do sound like a lunatic. I can hear the panic rising in my voice, and I can't do anything to stop it. "He can't stay here. There's nowhere for him to stay."

"What about your couch?"

I swear I can feel neurons exploding in my head, and my voice becomes unnaturally high. "*You want him to stay on my couch?*" Oh hell no. No, no, no, no. Just... *no.*

"Sure, why not? He won't bite."

But what if I want him to? The dirty thought rises unbidden. *In all the best places?* I press a hand to my suddenly hot cheek.

"Look. Just for a few weeks," Declan cajoles. "I've got some business to wrap up here, and then I'll be out for a visit. Was there anything else?" he adds after a pause.

Right. Visit. Business. I have *got* to get my head back into this conversation and stop thinking about Nico biting the inside of my thighs. I steel my voice. "The barrels in the cellar- do you know anything about them? How long they've been aging?"

"No idea."

I roll my eyes. Of course he doesn't. I've never met a vineyard owner so hands-off. On the one hand, I love it. If I work things right, I'm going to make my mark here and put us both on the radar. On the other? I wish to fuck I had someone, *anyone* to bounce the occasional idea off of. "No idea what grapes they are? Or if they're blended?"

"I assume Cab Sauv and Chardonnay?"

My thoughts too, given the grapes in the vineyard, but without a chemical analysis, there's no way to tell for sure. "Have you tasted them?"

"Have you?"

Hell yes, I have. "They're fucking amazing and they need to be released." I don't know who barreled them or when, but the person was genius, and the flavor is pure magic. Once I've identified what's in the barrel I want to get these to market as soon as possible. "Immediately," I add for emphasis.

"*What?* Can you even do that?"

I slowly count to five, because as much as I love my boss. Sometimes, he makes me crazy. "Look. You hired me to be the winemaker. I'm telling you, these are fantastic wines that we need to get to market. Yesterday."

"Okay, do it."

"Don't you want to come taste them?" I mean, what kind of owner releases something without at least tasting it

17

first? Even if he trusts his winemaker implicitly? *This is why I get paid the big bucks,* I think wryly.

"Look, I don't care if it's Cougar Juice. If you think it will make us money, get it to market."

Cougar Juice?!? That is the very last straw. "But you need to sign off on labels, on-on names. Fuck, Declan, you don't even have a name for the winery." My voice reaches hysteria level. *So* not professional, but how has the guy ended up a gazillionaire with this kind of attitude?

Privilege.

The word settles over me with a dull thud. Silly me. My heart briefly drops to my toes. He gives no shits whether this succeeds or not. Only I do. For the first time since I arrived in this mini-paradise, I feel utterly and truly alone.

"I'm paying you a fuck-ton of money to do this shit, Alison. I can't give this my attention right now. I trust you. Just run with it."

"Are you sure?" I ask, the fight gone out of me. I just want a final confirmation.

"You want that profit-share don't you? Do you trust your instincts?"

I sigh heavily, and stare down the hill at the undulating layers of fog. Truly? I do. But not this morning. Not while Nico Case is tied up on my couch. "Yeah, yeah. I do." Nothing like faking it until you make it.

"Great," Declan says enthusiastically. "Go for it. Look, my coffee's getting cold. Call if you have an emergency."

He hangs up. My boss fucking hangs up on me. No 'thanks, you're doing a great job,' not even a 'talk to you later.' I've been fucking dismissed to sort this out on my own. And sort it, I will. I may be stuck with Nico under-foot, but I'll be damned if I let him get under my skin. I am impervious. I'm fucking Teflon. I smile grimly as I jog back to the trailer. Nico Case has just met his match.

Chapter Four

Nico

*S*he bursts into the house like a fury, face flushed and filled with grim determination. I can practically see her wielding a sword instead of a frying pan. She looks me over, and damn, if I don't warm under her intense gaze.

I don't look away.

Instead, I study her now that she's dressed and not hiding her face under a blanket of beauty product. Her curves are just as enticing covered in athletic wear as they were in barely there lingerie. But it's her face that captivates me. The way her wide brown eyes spark with intelligence and curiosity. Her plump lips carry the hint of a smile- even while she glares at me. And her skin? Flawless. Like porcelain. Smooth and delicate with a kiss of pink high on her cheeks. I guess those beauty products work. Veronica always looked haggard without her 'face' on. I could stare at Alison all day, and still find something new to enchant me, like her perfectly shaped dark brows that add emphasis to whatever emotion is flitting through her head.

She clears her throat and heads for the kitchen, stopping to open a drawer. She returns with a pair of scissors, and for half a second, the thought of losing my balls makes me freeze like a deer in headlights. But the moment passes when she takes my wrists. Her touch is surprisingly gentle for someone who's bristling with energy. It's less gentle as she tears the tape from my wrists, catching some of my arm hair in the glue. "Ow!" I pull my hands away as soon as they're free.

The corner of her mouth lifts on one side. "It would have hurt worse if I'd tried to be tender."

"I don't think tender's in your vocabulary," I snap, wrists still stinging.

Her brow lifts, mimicking her mouth. "You'll never find out."

And suddenly, I want to. Could she be a tender lover, hands softly skating over my skin? Kissing slowly, rolling her hips languorously as I take her fully? Desire surges through me like an electric shock. I shift my hips, because there's no hiding the erection tenting my jeans like an over-sexed teenager.

"Stop squirming," she orders, yanking on the tape around my ankles.

"Yes ma'am," I retort, bringing my hands down to cover my junk, but fuck if that pressure doesn't arouse me further. As soon as my ankles are free, I swing my legs around to the floor, sending her scurrying across the room. "Don't worry," I mock. "I only bite when invited."

Her eyes jerk to mine, and again, I swear I see them stir with a molten heat that makes my blood run heavy and thick, straight to my balls. She props her hands on her hips. "I spoke with Declan."

I can't help the triumphant grin that pulls my mouth up. I lean back, clasping my hands behind my head.

Her eyes narrow to dark glittery points. "Don't look so smug. You might have use of my couch and my shower, but you'll also be putting in a full day's work for me. In the fields," she adds after a dramatic pause. Her expression dares me to disagree.

"I don't think so."

She shrugs. "Suit yourself. You'll need to be off the property in an hour, if that's the case. I've got a work crew showing up then and I can't be bothered to babysit you."

"You can't do that," I sputter, hands fisting and anger rising through me. "I'm an invited guest." Declan offered me a place to crash and now there are strings attached? So *fucking* typical with our family. Why am I even surprised?

She heads down the hall, not sparing me a glance. "Suit yourself." She disappears into her bedroom and shuts the door with a finality that echoes down the hall.

"Goddammit," I mutter, letting frustration get the best of me. She has me over a barrel and she knows it. Dec, too. I blame him as much as I blame her. Using me for free labor. I force my hands open. He wants to add insult to injury? *Fine.* Let him. I won't give him, or anyone else, the satisfaction of seeing me crumble. I may be down, I may be broke, but I am certainly not out. I rise and grab my backpack, fishing for my dopp kit. I brush my teeth in the kitchen sink, splash water on my face, and run my hands through my hair. This is as good as it gets right now, as good as it needs to get if I'm going to spend the day in the field.

Alison arches an eyebrow when she returns, looking more like a teenager in her overalls and work boots than a bonafide winemaker. I grudgingly give her props for wanting to be in the field. Plenty of winemakers leave the actual crop tending to their field crew, and swoop in at the end for the glamorous stuff. "Are you sure you want to wear those?" She eyes my Italian loafers dubiously.

I smile grimly. "Absolutely."

She shakes her head and mutters something under her breath that sounds a lot like 'princess' as she passes by and pushes through the front door. Her comment only strengthens my resolve. No one is going to be more surprised than Alison to discover I'm anything *but* a princess.

I follow her across the yard to the crushing barn, catching up to her as she reaches the big garage door. "Here, let me." I step around her and grab the handle, throwing my weight into the pull. Nothing. I try again, grunting from the effort.

"Are you done showing off yet?" She mocks with a note of laughter, as she unlocks the door to our right, and steps inside.

I hear a machine grind to life at the same time I hear the locks release on the garage door. Of course she keeps them locked. Fuck me.

She sticks her head back through the door, eyes twinkling. "You can be Hulk now." She disappears again and I throw open the wide door, which rolls up smoothly now that it's not locked. I let out a low whistle. Again, I'm impressed and mildly annoyed that Declan's scored such nice digs. The crushing pad looks newly renovated, the stainless tanks practically sparkle in the early morning sun.

"Nice, isn't it?" Alison says with appreciation, offering me a pair of work gloves. "This place is going to be hopping come harvest."

I make a noncommittal noise, not sure what to say. There's an air of festivity, of celebration that permeates every harvest, and even though it's been years since I've been close to the winemaking process, part of me still looks forward to the season. But chances are, I'll be gone long before harvest rolls around. At least that's my plan.

"In the corner behind the steel tanks are a couple of ten-gallon water dispensers. Can you fill them in the utility sink?"

I chafe at her request. Although she's nothing but polite, her tone of voice makes it clear I'm not to say no. *Karma...* the dark voice reminds me. There's no escaping it. I'm paying for my sins in a thousand different ways. I nod with a grunt and head off to find the water containers. When I return, Alison is passing out straw hats to a bunch of women gathered just under the garage door.

"*¡Oye! Señoras. Hoy tenemos que eliminar los brotas laterales, sí?*"

I have no idea what she's saying, but the women all nod their agreement.

She turns to the woman on her left. "*Carla, tú y yo, y Nico, vamos a inspeccionar la fruta y soltar el verde, bueno?*"

The woman named Carla turns and gives me a broad grin. "*Sí*"

"So did you just agree to feed me to the lions?" I ask when I'm within earshot of Alison.

She turns, and the playful smile on her face sends heat racing through me. "Maybe. Carla's definitely a lion, and if you don't... perform to expectations-" She smirks. "She might eat you alive."

I shoot a glance Carla's direction, trepidation rippling through me. Where did Alison find her? Or this crew, for that matter? All my years of growing up in Napa, I've never seen an entirely female crew. It must show on my face, because Alison scowls. "You have a problem taking orders from a bunch of women?"

I raise my hands in mock surrender. "I'm not really in a position to say, am I?"

She gives me a satisfied smile. "You and Carla and I are going down to the Cabernet lots to drop the green fruit."

"What's that?"

Alison's eyes grow wide. "The green drop? You don't know about the green drop?"

"Why should I?"

"Because you're a fucking Case, that's why. You of all people should know."

"Well, I don't," I snap, madly running through everything our head grower Morrie taught me about grape growing when I was a teenager. "I was the one being groomed to run the company one day, to make the big calls and delegate the rest. I didn't pay much attention to what was happening in the vineyard." The back of my neck heats under her shocked stare.

"Well it's high time you learned, pretty boy."

Anger sparks through me, making my fingers tingle. "Pretty boy?" My voice rises. "Where do you get off calling me pretty boy?"

Alison bites her lip, obviously trying not to laugh, and slides her gaze down to my shoes. I swear, it makes me want to shake her. Or kiss her. The latter thought jars me out of my anger for a split second. Strike that. I definitely don't want to kiss her. That mouth is entirely too sassy for my taste. A laugh escapes her anyway, and she shakes her head. "C'mon, Carla. Let's show Nico how it's done."

Carla gives an order to the crew. With nods and happy chatter, they take one of the water dispensers and head for the vines. Then she and Alison bend and begin to carry the other one, chattering away in Spanish. "Wait," I call after them, hurrying to catch up. "Let me carry that." They stop and drop the water tank, shooting amused glances at each other.

Alison shrugs. "Suit yourself."

They watch for a moment as I hoist up the barrel. It's heavy, but I've lifted heavier at the gym. Our gazes collide, mine triumphant, daring her to mock me. Hers- appreciative. And then she does that smirky, lip-bitey thing again and energy surges through me.

"Holler if you need to stop," she says before turning back to Carla, the two of them making their way into the vineyard.

"Don't worry," I call after them. "I've got this."

I've never regretted saying something more.

Chapter Five

Nico

*S*he didn't bother to tell me it was nearly a half-mile walk to the Cabernet lots. By the time we reach it, my shoulders are on fire, my biceps have seized, and I'm winded. This is the kind of shit Navy SEALS do-carrying over a hundred pounds for miles on end. Fuck me for trying to be a gentleman. I drop the barrel onto the picnic bench with a grunt, and flex my arms.

"You okay? Need a little water?" Alison teases with a giggle.

"I'm *fine.*" I growl. But I help myself anyway. A grappa-induced headache has started to form, and if I don't nip it in the bud, today will be worse than hell.

"Be sure to stay hydrated," Alison cautions. "It will feel cool, but we're working in direct sunlight."

I give her a salute and keep drinking.

She makes a frustrated noise in the back of her throat before turning to Carla and muttering some random shit I don't know in Spanish. Carla heads into the first row. Alison lays a hand on my arm and a shock reverberates through my bones. I'm instantly aware - of the coconut scent of her sunscreen, of the birds calling in the trees at the edge of the vineyard- everything comes into sharp relief. It's such a surprise, I miss what she's saying. "Come again?"

"I *said*, I'll show you what to do. I'm sure you'll catch on quickly. Follow me."

I follow her into the second row, my eyes drawn irresistibly to the sway of her luscious hips, and the hint of bare skin below her sports bra. She stops and hands me a pair of pruners. "What do you see?"

A breathtaking fresh-faced woman who against my better judgment, I want to kiss senseless.

I clear my throat. "Grapes."

She makes a face. "You have an amazing gift for the obvious."

For some reason that makes me laugh. It starts low in my belly and rises, bursting out in full peals. I bend, bracing my hands against my thighs. I haven't laughed in god knows how long, and it feels... good. Like something dark inside me has broken loose and evaporated.

"So glad to know you think that's funny," she states with a scowl, which only sets off another round of laughter.

I return upright and shoot her a grin. To my surprise, she smiles back. It's shy, sweet, even. Like I've broken through a layer of her defenses. We stare, and a current of electricity runs through my body. There's no denying the chemistry between us, and it unsettles me to my core. I clear my throat. "I see grapes at different stages of ripening."

This time, when she speaks, she's all business, and

whatever hovered in the air between us has dissipated. "Exactly. And come harvest time, greener grapes will negatively impact the flavor. Our job is to cut out the green."

"But that's going to lower your yield." And why would anyone in their right mind do that?

She gives me another withering stare. "Yes. It is."

I glower back. "But you're costing the vineyard money by doing that." I cross my arms. "And I know from experience, Dec doesn't like losing money."

"I'm making wine, not cougar juice."

"Cougar juice." What in the hell kind of fucked-up thing is that? Although from the disdain in her voice, I have a feeling it's nothing good.

She laughs derisively. "C'mon, pretty boy, you've had to have heard that term- it's what everyone calls your wines."

Now I'm pissed. "No way. We have a reputation for making California's premier wines." At least we did. When I was a kid. To be honest, all I've done is crunch numbers with the express intent of increasing yield and profits. I haven't given much thought to the wine. Why would I? We've always hired winemakers to oversee the flavor.

She lifts her eyes skyward with a shake of her head before staring at me hard. "Wake up and smell the coffee, Nico... Case Wineries makes party wine. Overripe, overpriced jammy fruitbombs that the ladies drink to get hammered. No subtlety. No terroir. No craft. Certainly nothing a winemaker of any caliber would want to stake their reputation on."

Her words sting, but deep down inside, I recognize a ring of truth. There comes a point where all empires run the risk of becoming too big and collapsing in on themselves. Is that what's happened to my family's empire? That would explain Dad's recent insanity regarding his legacy.

But I don't want to lose this battle. I've been groomed

since I was twelve to call the shots. "And what makes you think you're going to do better by Dec?" I say with a pointed glare.

She glares back. "He hired me to make the best wine I can, and I'm going to do just that. With or without you."

"So you're giving me an ultimatum. You won't even listen to reason."

"It's my job to make wine, not to coddle entitled rich boys going through a midlife crisis."

"I'm *not-*" but I stop, because she's right. I sound like a petulant four-year-old who hasn't gotten his way. "Fine," I say, swallowing hard. "It's your funeral." She may have won this round, but I'm damn well gonna make sure she makes Dec a return on his investment.

Triumph flickers in her eyes, and her mouth pulls into a smirk. "Maybe it's my party. Now," she says brusquely, dusting her hands together. "As I was saying- We need to drop the green fruit, so the clusters ripen evenly." She narrows her eyes. "So that we can sell our wine for a premium."

I make a point of ignoring the dig. "Great." I swoop down to a cluster of mostly green grapes, pruners open.

"Wait." Her hand comes to my arm again. "Not so fast."

For a hot second my mind goes blank. This woman drives me nuts. For starters, she's crazy-pants. Bossy. Opinionated. Yet I can't deny the zip of electricity racing up my arm. It warms my body in ways I don't recall experiencing- with Veronica or anyone else. And for a stupid second, I wonder what it would be like to be on the receiving end of that kind of touch all the time.

"We need to make sure the vines are balanced, that the clusters aren't too close together. Likewise, if you see grapes that are too red, that are, ah-"

"Too excited?" I give her a sideways glance.

Her cheeks turn the color of clouds at dawn. "Sure. Too excited," she repeats with a breathy note. "We need to thin those too."

"So this one." I point to a cluster with my pruners. "Would you drop this?"

"I would."

I glance her direction again. "Is there anything else I need to know?"

Her eyes flick to mine, and for a long moment neither of us speak. She shakes her head. "T-that's all. I'll work the other side." She turns, but not before I see the flush deepening on her face.

We set to work, and for the first hour, we don't speak except for when I ask the occasional question about a cluster. The trees are alive with bird calls, and the breeze dances lightly through the vines. By the end of the first row, I'm dripping, and I remove my shirt. Alison works faster than me, but by the end of the second row, I've matched my pace to hers. "Here," I say roughly, handing her a plastic cup filled with water when we're midway down the fourth row. "You need to drink, too."

She tucks her pruners into a loop on her overalls and accepts my offering, gulping half of it before stopping to take a breath. "You want some?"

I shake my head. "Took my fill at the picnic table."

She drains the cup, and I watch, mesmerized by the undulating movement in her throat. It's so erotic, so sensual, my breath catches in my clavicle. "Give it to me," I say with a little too much grit in my voice. She drops the cup into my hand, and I spin and hoof it down the row back to the table. I have no business lusting after Alison Walker.

By the time Alison makes the call to break for lunch,

my body is on fire. My shoulders ache, my arms feel like lead, and I'm pretty sure I'll never be able to open my hands again. One of the crewwomen has brought down a cooler and placed it next to the water dispensers on the picnic table, and the ladies dig in, passing out sandwiches and fruit. Alison motions me forward. "Help yourself."

I peer into the cooler. There's only one sandwich and an apple remaining. I glance back at Alison. It hits me that she hadn't planned on feeding an extra person. "You take it," I say with a shake of my head.

She crosses her arms across her chest, accentuating the deep vee of her cleavage and making me hungry for something other than food. "I've never had crew pass out on me before, and I'm sure as hell not going to start now."

"And I'm not an asshole," I retort. The arch of her brow implies she thinks otherwise. Something catches deep in my chest. I don't like that this perfect stranger has already weighed me in the balance and found me wanting. "I'm not," I reiterate firmly. "And I'm not going to let a woman go hungry while I eat."

Her eyes spark with challenge. "So if I was a man ordering you to eat up, you'd have no problem?"

Fuck.

"Spare me your gentlemanly posturing." She glares at me, widening her stance just slightly, as if she's ready to do battle. "My crew eats first. Period."

I mimic her stance, crossing my arms. "No. You need to eat, too."

Her eyes narrow, and for a second, I think she's going to give in. Then my stomach growls loudly. I haven't eaten since sometime yesterday, and I'm starving, but she's got to be hungry too. I didn't see her eat breakfast, either. "Last call, pretty boy," she says in a low voice, brimming with anger. It's the kind of tone that says *don't fuck with me*, and I can't resist fucking with her.

"Take it," I say with a wave.

She reaches into the cooler and grabs the apple, tossing it to Carla, then lifts out the sandwich. "*Alguien?*" she asks, looking around at the women assembled in a half-circle.

One of the older women pushes forward a girl who looks barely sixteen. "*Mi hija tiene hambre.*"

Alison hands her the sandwich, and she ducks her head in gratitude. But instead of diving in, she pulls half from the wax bag and shares it with the older woman. The others cluck their approval as the sandwich gets demolished. As I watch the women circle Alison for directions on what's next, I'm surprised by the hollow feeling in my chest. This was an empty victory, if you could even call it that, and I came off looking like an ass. I hover on the outskirts as she speaks to the women in Spanish. When they disband, she glares at me and waves a hand toward the end of the picnic bench. "We need to gather up the droppings for mulch. Baskets are there. We'll haul them up top to the mulch piles."

"You should bring the flatbed truck down here." I saw there was one behind the barn, and even I know it's meant for work like this. "It would be easier to load it up then drive it straight to the compost."

"The hike too much for you, pretty boy?"

I scoff. "No. I just think it's a waste of manpower to have a dozen of us do the work a truck could do. Much better use of your dollars."

Alison levels a smoldering glare at me. "And maybe, I don't want diesel fumes anywhere near my vines."

"Suit yourself," I grumble and grab a basket.

We spend the next hour hauling buckets full of grape and leaf matter uphill to three enormous compost piles behind the barn. The women chatter back and forth merrily, hardly sparing me a glance, while I become grouchier with each laborious step uphill. *How the mighty have fallen*, the dark voice inside my head taunts. Like any of this was my doing. Except that I was complicit, the infuriatingly pragmatic part of me points out. I took advantage of a situation to exact payback from Jason. I let myself get pulled into a loveless marriage and let Ronnie spend my trust fund indiscriminately so she'd leave me alone. I believed Dad when he promised that I would head Case Family Wineries someday. So this hell is all of my making, which only serves to darken my mood and add to the lead weight pulling on my bones as I blister my hands lugging buckets up and down a hill like a common laborer. At least they're getting paid.

My head is throbbing when I stop for water, and the first thing I do is dump a full cup over my head. The icy cold takes my breath away, but then it's nothing but sweet relief as my head and neck cool. I dump a second cup over my head, welcoming the icy blast this time as the water drips down my torso.

Behind me, Alison clears her throat. I turn to catch her staring, eyes smoldering with hunger. My body answers with a thrill of awareness, and I stare back, equally hungry. The air between us crackles with tension, an electrifying mix of mutual attraction and dislike.

She coughs and glares. "I want you to head into St. Helena. I have an account set up at Central Valley. Pick yourself up some suitable clothes."

"But the others aren't done."

Alison looks pointedly at my feet, and my gaze follows hers. My shoes are trashed. The supple Italian leather is covered with a thick layer of dirt, and one of the seams has split. My designer jeans have fared little better.

"I'm not stopping until they are," I answer stubbornly.

"You've done enough for today." Her tone of voice implies that I've hardly done anything.

"How can you say that?" I sputter. "I've worked my ass off."

"Do you want a cookie for your efforts?" Her plump mouth thins. "You need to leave now, or the store will be closed, and I can't have you prancing around the vineyard tomorrow like a dilettante."

"I do not prance."

The corner of her mouth slowly kicks up. "Oh you most definitely prance, pretty boy, and I can't have my workers distracted by your fine moves."

There's a compliment in there, somewhere, more than one, and my chest puffs at the knowledge she's been checking me out. I flex and swivel my hips. "You mean these fine moves?" My smartassery earns me nothing more than a scathing glare. She turns and marches back to the vines. I can't resist calling after her. "I'll show you my best moves when I get back."

She flips me the bird and keeps going. For the second time today, laughter erupts from deep in my belly. Alison Walker is a ball buster. No doubt about it, and surprisingly, I find that sexy as fuck.

Chapter Six

Nico

*I*t's hours later, when I finally return, dusty, exhausted, and desperately in need of a shower. And given the way today went, it wouldn't surprise me if Alison insisted I bathe with the hose inside the crushing pad. All afternoon, I've been itchy and tense. Filled with an electric kind of agitation that even a leisurely ride down the winding roads of Mt. Veeder doesn't calm.

I pause at the trailer door, hand resting on the handle. Should I knock? Fuck no, I reprimand myself. Alison may not like that she has a house guest, but for the time being, this is my place and I have every right to come and go as I please. Without knocking, I burst into the living room and drop my sack of new clothes on the floor.

"Don't *do* that," Alison yelps, jumping back from the stove.

Something clatters to the floor, and I'm instantly aware of several things. First, the aroma filling the space is

35

mouthwatering. Whatever she's cooking is loaded with garlic, and my stomach gives a loud grumble. I'm famished and I could eat everything. Including Alison, who looks downright edible in leggings and a dark pink drapey top with the shoulders cut out. It clings to her curves, and I itch to run my hands over her softness. Her hair is down, falling in flowing waves past her shoulders. A carafe of white wine stands on the table, which has been set for two.

"The shower is in my room," she states, concentrating on stirring whatever's in the pan. "There's a washer in the hall. Although you might want to burn what you're wearing." She refuses to look my direction.

I shuck my leather jacket, and toss it over the arm of the couch.

"There's a closet next to the washer," she says with a note of irritation. "You can hang your jacket there."

"Anal retentive, much?" I retort.

"My house, my rules," she snaps back, stirring vigorously.

"Whatever you say, your highness," I say with a mock bow. Irritated she won't even glance at me. Whatever. Living with a woman I don't like isn't anything new. Only it eats at me this time, because we shared a smile in the vineyard, and I assumed it meant she didn't hate my guts. *Dumbass.* I hang my jacket and dump my shoes in the wastebasket. There's no salvaging them. Alison's bedroom is as immaculate as the rest of the house, and I hesitate in the doorway, surveying the giant king-sized bed with navy and gray silk sheets. Sheets that are meant to be rumpled, twisted, and yanked during a session of heavy lovemaking. My cock swells, pressing against my zipper at the thought of messing those perfectly tucked in sheets, of seeing Alison flushed and spread out in the middle of the bed, ready to be fucked into next week.

Shoving the thought aside, and forcing my dick to calm down, I cross the room, and enter the bathroom. And fuck me if it's not resplendent in femininity. As austere as the bedroom is, the bathroom is another case entirely. Bottles, pots, and potions line the countertop, arranged by size and color, a stack of fluffy white towels fills a gold shelf, and a pink satin robe hangs on a hook. I reach out to finger the material. Silk. I shut my eyes as my cock jumps eagerly at the vision of the material gliding across her curves, teasing her nipples into hard peaks. I bite back a groan. This room screams sensuality, and pleasure. I'm half tempted to check her drawers for a dildo. What other secrets does Alison harbor in what is clearly her sanctuary?

My fingers twitch, and my pulse races at what I'm about to do. I know it's wrong, invasive. But I want to know. Fuck, I haven't been curious to actually *know* a woman in... maybe ever. But Alison has clearly wormed her way under my skin, and I desperately want to discover what makes her tick. In spite of the fact I hear her banging away in the kitchen, I look over my shoulder, guilt gnawing at me for what I'm about to do. I slide open the first drawer. No surprises there- a toothbrush, toothpaste, floss. A tube of zit cream. A razor. Fuck, does she shave her pussy? Another image rises, unbidden, of a slick, smooth pussy, swollen and waiting for my touch.

I shut the drawer and move to the next. My stomach jumps when I see the contents. I've hit the jackpot, but it's not at all what I expected. No dildo, or lipstick vibe, no handcuffs or naughty toys- only a pile of sticky notes. I glance at the mirror and can see the vague outline of glue around the perimeter. She obviously didn't want me to see these. I'm surprised she didn't mind me seeing the softer side of her on display and wildly curious to discover what she felt necessary to hide. I grab the pile, flipping through as my stomach yo-yos with each brightly colored note.

This body is just the keeper of my magic
My body is not an apology
*I **LOVE** my curves*
My body is strong and resilient
DO WHAT MATTERS- FOCUS ON WHAT MATTERS
I am a strong, sexy, beautiful Asian American woman
You are the new hotness

Fuck. *Fuckfuckfuck.* I drop the notes, heart slamming against my ribs, and shut the drawer a little too forcefully. My stomach churns at how I've violated Alison's privacy. I don't deserve to know the secret side of her, what makes her lose sleep at night, what feeds her insecurity. But there's no unseeing those words, or the loopy, clearly emotional handwriting. My cheeks heat with shame that runs straight to my toes. I'm half-tempted to hop on my motorcycle and disappear. I know how to keep secrets. Dark ones, shameful ones- the kind that are best forgotten and never allowed to see the light of day. I don't know how to keep secrets of the heart, secrets laced with hope, with determination. Her secrets scare me, because there's more than shame at stake. There's a heart.

I blow out a breath through puffed cheeks and quickly shed my clothes, turning the water to scalding, once again wondering if I can possibly scrub the filth from my soul. But rose-scented soap and rough washcloths aren't enough, and when the water starts to cool, I exit, feeling as dirty and dark as when I stepped in. Too late, I realize my new wardrobe is still in the living room. I wrap the towel around my hips and head for the living room. There's no chance I can get to my clothes without Alison noticing, so I might as well own it and see if I can get a rise from her in the process.

"Dinner's rea-" she turns, words dying on her lips when she takes in my towel. Her eyes darken to nearly black as she stares avidly. My balls turn heavy and full under her gaze, filled with an ache desperate for release. She licks her lips, then seems to shake herself. "Please get dressed," she orders primly as she returns to the stove, and busies herself filling our plates.

"I'm pretty comfortable like this," I drawl, smirking at the way her back stiffens.

"If you're expecting a compliment," she bites out, "you're sadly mistaken."

I flex and grin when I catch her sneaking a peek my direction. "The fact that it seems like you're bent on seducing me is compliment enough."

She gasps and slams her spatula on the counter, cheeks flushing as pink as her pretty top. "I am *not* doing anything of the kind."

"Oh?" I drop into one of the chairs at the table. The towel pops open at the bottom exposing part of my thigh.

She turns, eyes shooting daggers, but her mouth drops open when she fixates on my leg. She grabs a shallow breath, eyes narrowing to glittering points. "Are you trying to get kicked out? Because I don't give a shit what Declan says. Any more of these-these *shenanigans*, and so help me, I will boot you out in nothing but what you're wearing."

"So explain to me the nice dinner, the wine…" I wave at the carafe on the table. "And the jazz coming from your phone." I've got her here, and she knows it.

She huffs out a breath. "Contrary to what you might

think, *some* women do this kind of thing for themselves, and not because they're hoping to get laid," she says with a tone as sharp as glass. Her eyes turn icy. "I can't force you to put on pants, but I refuse to serve food to Neanderthals. If you want to eat, *put on a damned shirt.*"

I rub a hand across my pecs. "But the view won't be as nice," I tease.

"*I'll. Live,*" she grits, clearly at the end of her patience.

"Your loss," I say with an overly dramatic sigh.

"Not really," she snaps back. "I value more than a hot body."

"So you're saying I'm hot?" I flex again as I rise and take the few steps to where my bag lies next to the door.

"I'm saying I don't give a shit about bodies."

"I call bullshit." I pull a black tee over my head. "Everyone wants hot bods." I roll my shoulders back to stretch the cotton, and turn, catching Alison with an almost forlorn expression on her face. My stomach sinks. I've gone too far.

Her jaw sets as her eyes bore straight into my soul. "Wrong. Everyone wants someone who's not a douchebag."

Ouch. But I can't say I didn't deserve that. Her arrow hit its mark right in the middle of my chest. Tension fills the space between us, and even though it's not in my nature to apologize, I see the words on the stickies. "I'm sorry. I went too far," I say in a low voice.

She swallows visibly and nods. "Let me get your plate."

"Let me," I offer. "You sit."

"No, I-"

"*Sit,*" I order, sidestepping her and moving to the stove. She's baked salmon, sautéed broccoli rabe with garlic, and cooked a steaming pot of herbed rice. "Holy shit, this looks amazing."

She makes a disbelieving noise in the back of her throat. "I thought it would go well with the wine."

I turn with two plates piled high. "So what other hidden talents do you have, Alison?" Veronica couldn't be bothered to lift a finger, let alone cook. I can't remember the last time someone cooked a nice meal for me. I know she said she eats this way all the time, and maybe she does, but her effort feels... personal. And I'm grateful.

Her cheeks turn that pretty shade of pink again, and she turns quickly, reaching for the carafe and pouring out the wine. "So I found these barrels in the cellar, and this wine comes from one of them." Her voice rises two tones and goes breathy at the end.

She's not used to compliments. "Tell me more," I ask as I set the plates down and take a seat.

"I assume your palate is fairly developed. Taste it."

The glass holds a full pour, so I can't really swirl it, but I do gently circle the glass to catch a whiff of the aroma. "I smell apples and buttery toasty notes. The color is deeper than straw, indicating some age."

Alison makes a noncommittal noise and nods, leaning forward in her chair. "Taste it."

There's anticipation in her voice, an eagerness I haven't heard before, and again, I can't help but wonder what this woman is like when she's aroused. I take a sip, letting the wine sit on my tongue a long moment before I swallow. I'm hit with bright notes of stone fruit, with a creamy luscious mouthfeel. It's fucking phenomenal. "Neutral oak?" I ask, keeping my cards close for the moment.

"Tastes like it, doesn't it? There's no record."

"You're kidding."

She gives me a baleful look. "I wouldn't kid about something this good." She takes a sip, and the pleasure on her face as she experiences the wine is nothing short of arousing. I'm grateful for the table between us as my cock tents my towel. She opens her eyes, excitement written all over her face. "This wine is fanfuckingtastic," she says breaking into a grin.

I raise my glass. "To fanfuckingtastic wine."

"I'll cheers to that." She clinks her glass against mine and takes another sip. She takes up her fork, and tries a bite of the salmon, slowly chewing, and then finishing with another taste of the wine. "I knew it," she says, flushing with excitement. "I *knew* this would be perfect with salmon."

You're so beautiful when you're excited.

She drops her fork, freezing, hand in midair.

Fuck, did I say that out loud? The expression on her face says I did. Fuck. *Fuckfuckfuck.*

Chapter Seven

Alison

"You're so beautiful when you're excited."

I freeze, my fork slipping from my fingers, emotions flooding my body. Nico's earlier comment rings in my head. *Everyone wants a hot bod.* No shit, Sherlock. Tell me something I don't know. I was foolish enough to believe that was different, once upon a time. I know better now.

He must be punking me. My *bod* is the furthest thing from hot, and it's certainly not beautiful. *I'm* not beautiful. I can never *be* beautiful. Not in this body. How many times did Tommy shout at me, voice dripping with disdain, that I was butt-ugly? That if I had any self-respect, I'd go to the gym and lose a few pounds. How many times did Nico and his cohort call me worse?

I'll settle for 'not-ugly'. I'll settle for healthy. And maybe someday I can look into the mirror and believe the affirmations I recite off of pretty-colored stickies every time I look in the mirror. But beautiful? Never. It's not in my vocabulary.

Shame burns in my chest, racing up my neck and heating my face.

Nico's face registers surprise, then his brows knit together. "What? Did I offend you?"

"Don't fuck with me," I say, voice shaking. "And for fuck's sake, don't insult me by saying shit you don't mean," I bite, the old anger rising up. I won't tolerate taunts in my own house. Not anymore. I fight the urge to run. If one of us is leaving, it's Nico. He can use his goddamn motorcycle as a pillow for all I care.

He glares back. "I don't fuck with people."

"Bullshit," I counter. "You're a Case. That's what you do."

His jaw tightens, and he grips his fork so hard his knuckles turn white. But he squirms in his seat, guilt flashing across his face before he breaks eye contact. "Not anymore," he mumbles.

Jesus. Does he remember? My stomach drops. That's a conversation I'm far from ready to have.

He grabs his wine and takes a big gulp. Sinfully large for the kind of wine we're drinking.

"Hey, that's not a wine cooler," I snap, covering up my feelings of helplessness and discomfort with aggression.

He slams the glass on the table so hard, some of the wine sloshes out, then stares me down with fire in his eyes. "I'll freely admit I'm an asshole, and someday, we can decide to unpack all the ways I deserve to go to hell, but I am most definitely *not* fucking with you, Alison."

I want to believe him. The way he says my name makes my pussy ache. God, I want to believe him so bad. But I can't purge the memories. Or the shame that goes with them.

He makes an animal noise of pure frustration. A completely male, testosterone-filled, sexy as fuck noise, and he rises. "I'm. Not. Fucking. With. You." He articulates and pushes back from the table to stand.

His words only register in the back of my brain, because all I can see is the enormous erection tenting the towel slung low across his hips. My breath sticks in my throat. I'm hallucinating. I must be. Because the man is hung like a fucking horse. My fingers twitch, because fuck, I want to grab it, run my hands along his length. *Taste it.* I flick my gaze to his. His hazel eyes burn me, and the heat sears me all the way to my pussy. My clit throbs, dying for touch, and I can feel the desire rising through me. I want to run, to step outside and gulp cool air. I have to gain some kind of control, because my brain cells are exploding at an alarming rate, making it difficult to breathe, let alone stand.

"You're lying," I whisper.

He closes the space between us, and my heart jumps to my throat as he pulls me up from my chair. His hand engulfs mine, his thumb caressing the place where my callouses live under my skin. His touch is too much. My nipples tingle, hardening to bullets, aching for pinches and licks, for everything my dirty mind has ever fantasized about. He brings my hand to his cock, and oh dear lord, I can feel the lip of his crown, the searing heat of him through my 900 GSM towel.

"Dicks never lie, angel."

My heart is pumping so hard, I think I might faint. What kind of a desperate maniac does it make me that all I can think of is *how bad* I want that cock inside me, filling me up?

He tangles his fingers in my hair, tilting my face up. "At least let me kiss you," he murmurs.

I must be imagining things, because I swear, there's a note of desperation in his voice. The rational part of me is screaming for me to put a stop to this. "I don't like you," I confess.

He lets out a dry laugh, his breath skating across my cheek and sending goosebumps down my neck and across my collarbone. "I'm not sure I like you either, but I can't stop thinking about fucking you."

"That's quite possibly the hottest thing anyone's ever said to me," I murmur, past the point of filtering my speech.

"I can say hotter," he murmurs, dipping his head and taking my mouth.

I'm utterly unprepared for the riot of energy that assaults me. The time I zapped myself plugging in a curling iron with damp fingers doesn't begin to hold a candle to the jolt of heat and electricity that hits me everywhere at once. Like, I think I literally fried my circuit board, and if I ever speak coherently again, it will be a miracle.

His mouth is alternately soft and coaxing, then fierce and demanding, his tongue taking ownership of my mouth, demanding my submission, and in spite of my rational self freaking out, I fall into the kiss, letting the sensations roll over me and pull me under. He kisses me like he's desperate, like he wants me naked, like I'm his last breath, his last... everything. And how can a woman not respond to that? I sink into the sensation, forgetting every-thing except the feeling of his tongue against mine, losing myself in the swirl of neurons exploding.

I give his cock a tentative squeeze, and he groans into my mouth. That's all the encouragement I need, and for a hot second, I completely forget myself, stroking him through the towel I'm not quite brave enough to remove.

"Tell me you have condoms stashed someplace," he murmurs as he relinquishes my mouth.

The words act like ice-water. I can't deny I want him too, but the rational, protective part of me, still holds sway. *But it's been so long,* the wanton side of me argues. For a beautiful second, I give in to lust. But then my courage vanishes. Fuck, who'm I kidding? I can't do this. "I can't have orgasms," I mumble, face burning. "Not during sex," I clarify. I've got a two-hundred dollar vibrator that does the trick quite nicely. But with a man? Even a woman—because, yes, after my divorce, I swung the other way for a while, desperate to figure out what was wrong with me. Never. Never with another human.

Nico's voice is the picture of disbelief. "Now *you're* bull-shitting me."

I shake my head, averting my eyes. "I think there's something wrong with your dick."

"There's nothing the fuck wrong with my dick, angel," he grits, thrusting into my hand.

No. No, there's *definitely* not anything wrong with his dick. Kill me now. He closes the remaining space between us, pinning my hand between my very soft hips, and his angular, hard ones.

"Your partners should burn in hell for leaving you high and dry."

I'm touched by his ferocity, yet I still don't trust it. "Comes with the territory," I mumble.

"Bullshit," he grits, crooking a finger under my chin and forcing my gaze to his.

I blink rapidly, fighting the tears that have suddenly flooded my eyes. I don't want to be this honest. *Especially* with someone like Nico. I can't let him see me cry. I swallow and clamp down on the riot of emotions tumbling through me. "Have you noticed I'm fat?" I say baldly, unable to disguise the despair in my voice.

"Have you noticed, I don't give a shit? You're sexy as fuck, Alison." He thrusts into my hand again, for emphasis. "Feel that? That's me, desperate to fuck your brains out."

My mouth curls up of its own accord. "You're not the desperate type."

He huffs out a low laugh. "Apparently, tonight I am."

"But your ex-wife," I mumble, throwing up my last defense.

"Is a lying, cheating, stealing, bitch on wheels who I hope I never see again."

"Oh." I let out a sigh. *It would have been easier to leave Tommy if he'd cheated.*

He shakes his head and steps back, holding up his hands. I feel the loss of him keenly. "Forget I said anything," he says, eyes turbulent. "I didn't mean to offend you."

"No." I close the space between us, my hand irresistibly drawn back to his erection. "You didn't offend me. It's… it's just…" I take a big breath. "I've been burned. It's hard for me to take people at face value."

His face shutters. "You're not the only one who's been burned, sweetheart." He stares down at me, eyes dark and dangerous. "And if you keep stroking me like that, I'm gonna jizz all over this towel."

I giggle. I've been unable to stop squeezing him and stroking him while we argue, because Christ, his cock is magnificent. "I don't have condoms," I confess.

"Condoms aren't necessary for orgasms. Only sex," he says without missing a beat. "Say the word, and I'll give you as many orgasms as you want."

My heart is pounding so loudly, I'm sure Nico can hear it, too. Saying yes is dangerous. But the thought of orgasms with another human makes my mouth water. My mind goes to the stack of affirmations I've hidden in my bathroom drawer. *I am the new hotness. I am strong and sexy.* There's no need to apologize for my urges. Years of therapy have taught me that, even if I still have trouble embracing it. I suck in a breath and slide my hand up his cock then hook my fingers inside the towel. The towel drops to the floor with only a gentle tug. His crown is dark pink and slick with pre-come. He half-growls, half-groans from the back of his throat and the sound arrows through me, straight to my aching pussy. I coat my thumb in his arousal, then bring it to my tongue. The salty tang explodes on my tongue, and I'm instantly addicted. I could taste him for days and not be satisfied.

"Alison," he says tightly.

I sense the barely leashed control, and also a plea- for what I don't know. But tonight, I'm firing my rational self, and I'm going to take all this man will give me. I stand on tiptoe, offering my mouth, while still caressing the tip of him. "Yes," I murmur. "Yes to everything."

Chapter Eight

Nico

*S*he's killing me. I don't think I've ever felt close to dying before, but I'm quite sure this is what it feels like. My balls are heavy and tight, and if she keeps teasing my cock with her sexy fingers, I'm gonna blow like a goddamned teenager the first time he sees pussy.

I nearly do just that when she licks my pre-come off her thumb. Her eyes are dark pools of desire. I can see the unabashed want there and I hold my breath, waiting for her answer, praying to any god that will listen. I don't deserve anything good in my life. I've taken too much, hurt too much, but I find myself bargaining that I'll be better if she just says yes. "Alison," I beg, not even sure what I'm begging for, except relief from the tension spooling through me, driving me to the edge of insanity.

It's blessed relief when she offers her mouth with a simple, "Yes. Yes to everything."

I snake my arm around her, pulling her flush against me as I take her mouth, claiming it with a hungry groan. There is no question that I will be claiming the rest of her, inch by lovely inch. I want to hear my name on her lips, begging for more, begging for release. I want to see her flushed and languid in the aftermath of multiple orgasms.

She kisses me back with an enthusiasm that only ratchets the ache in my balls, my need for release. I bend, and sweep her into my arms. Alison is not a delicate flower, she's… substantial, but I don't care. Her curves drive me wild, and the words of her hidden affirmations keep bouncing around my head.

"What are you doing?" she gasps, tearing her mouth from mine. "Put me down. You'll hurt-"

"Hush," I order, taking her mouth again. My arms may be on fire from the day's labor, but I'm not a pussy. I can bench two-fifty, and she's not anywhere close to that. I carry her the dozen or so steps down the hall, kick open the door to her bedroom, and place her on the bed. "Clothes off, angel," I say as I pull my shirt over my head and drop it to the floor. "I refuse to be the only one with no clothes."

Her eyes widen and turn hungry as she scans my body. She reaches out and traces my abs. It takes effort, but I hold absolutely still, letting her take her fill of my body. I can't wait to do the same with her. Her hand dips between my legs to cup my balls. My cock jerks, the tip weeping for her touch, for her mouth.

"Alison," I say roughly. "Take your fucking clothes off."

Her mouth breaks into a slow, dirty smile at my crudeness, eyes lighting with expectation. "Or what?"

"I will tear that pretty pink blouse in two," I promise, half-hoping she pushes me to keep my word.

"Yeah?"

Fuck, I love how she doesn't give an inch. "Try me."

She leans back on her elbows, biting her lip, eyes daring me to make good on my promise.

I bend and brace my hands on either side of her elbows, looming over her. My blood runs heavy and thick through my veins, pulsing in time with my cock. The animal part of my brain has taken over. I want to roar, to rut like a bull and mark her everywhere. I nip at her lower lip, biting just hard enough to elicit a gasp, then soothe it with my tongue. She lifts her head, chasing my mouth. I let her catch me- it's no hardship to have her mouth on mine, her tongue sliding against mine with needy abandon. I could kiss her all night, but there are other pleasures to be had.

Our heavy breaths echo off the walls, filling the room with an ancient, primal music. I trace a finger along her neckline, searching for a weakness in the fabric, which I find close to her shoulder. I rise, bringing both hands to the seam and I pull, hard. The fabric rends with a treble screech, ripping the fabric in a diagonal slash, exposing a thin lace bra, see through enough that I can see her dark nipples puckered and tight.

I yank again, reducing her shirt to shreds and pulling the pieces off until she's in nothing but her sexy lace bra. I give a silent fist pump when I see it's a front clasp. I drop my mouth to her nipple, licking and biting at it through the fabric until she writhes beneath me. I give the other the same treatment. My cock is like steel, and grinding into the soft silky bedspread offers no relief. But right now, this isn't about me. I reach for the clasp and pop it open, her breasts spill out of the fabric in the most magnificent fashion. I dive in like a man starved- licking, biting, leaving my mark on the satiny, soft flesh, that I can't get enough of.

Her breath has turned to pants, her moans to mewling cries.

I reach for the edge of her leggings. Her hand covers mine, and I raise my head. Her face is glorious, cheeks flushed, eyes glazed, lips plump and bruised, her chest red where my stubble has grazed her skin. "Are you okay?" I rasp.

She bites her lip, panic momentarily flashing across her face. She drags in a ragged breath.

"Do you want me to stop?"

She shakes her head vehemently. "No. I-I..." she pulls in another uneven breath. "Don't stop. Please," she adds after a moment, pushing on the elastic and lifting her hips.

Please has never sounded more beautiful. I yank her pants over her hips, and in seconds, they join my shirt on the floor. She wears high-waisted sheer lace panties that match her bra, but what has me riveted is the dark stain of arousal at her pussy. I drop my head to the spot and inhale deeply, filling my lungs with the sweet musky scent of her. She tastes just as lovely, and I tongue and suck at the fabric, filling myself with her.

She lets out a long sigh and an "Oooooooooohhhhhh," that ends in a moan.

"You'll like it even better with your pants off," I rasp.

She answers with a vocal sigh. "Yes."

Shamelessly, I bring my hands to the seam and rip, the sound of fabric tearing cutting through our breathless pants. The other side tears just as easily, and then she's free. Exposed to my gaze, pussy lips swollen and deep pink, peeking out through a neatly trimmed triangle of dark hair. It takes all my self-control to not dive in and feast. But I want this to be unforgettable for her. Permanently etched into her brain for the rest of her life. I drop to my knees and push her thighs open.

Alison's head pops up. "What are you- *oooohhhh.*" She moans when I trace my tongue up the inside of her thigh. "Are you sure you- OOhhh," she moans again when I bite at the juncture of her inner thigh and torso- a breath from her pussy.

Her hips rock as I mark her thighs, and one of her hands clutches at my hair. The other grabs at the bedspread. "Do you want me to taste your pretty cunt, angel?"

"Yes," she says between pants, spreading her legs wider. I bring my hands to her cunt, gently exposing the most private part of her. She unfurls like a flower- an exotic lily, with deep red lips fading to dark pink and light brown, glistening with arousal. Her clit is stiff and dark, emerging from its hood like a rosebud in spring. I want to claim this part of her, mark it as my own. My mouth and fingers will have to suffice for now, but soon enough, my cock will take this, fill her like she's never been filled before.

I draw a finger from the dark pucker at her ass, over the soft flesh to her opening. I circle it slowly, paying attention to her breath, to the way she moves, watching for clues about what she likes, how she wants to be touched. I dip a finger into her opening, coating my finger in her honey. "Do you like how this feels?"

"Yes. Oh *god* yes," she gasps, arching into my finger.

"And what about this?" I slide my finger upward and circle her clit, finishing with a little pinch.

Her hips buck off the bed. Her breath is ragged, shallow, barely in control. My scalp tingles from the ferocity of her hair pulling. "Yesss. Oh that, too."

I drop my mouth to the inside of her thigh again. "You want my mouth on that gorgeous cunt?"

"Yes."

My mouth hovers over her pussy, not close enough to

touch, but close enough she feels my breath where she wants my mouth. "Do you want me to eat it until you come? Until you can't think?"

She pulls on my hair so hard, my eyes water. "*Yes,*" she growls. "Stop talking."

I've never been happier to oblige. I take a long slow swipe up her seam, tasting her, committing her flavor to memory. She's like a fine wine, complex and luscious. She fills my mouth with notes of salt, musk, and a sweetness that's uniquely her. I lick again, exploring every dip and crevice, every crenulation. Her hips take on a rhythm that I match as I slowly devour her, saving her clit for last. I can tell from her cries and the way she writhes, that she's close, but I'm so far from finished, it's not funny. I dip my tongue into her channel, thrusting with the same slow, relentless pace I plan to use when I finally fuck her, losing myself in her flavor, sucking and licking like she's my last meal. She lets out a long, low moan when I finally seal my mouth over her clit, lapping at the rigid point like a cat with cream. Her cries rise and her thighs squeeze my head in a vice-like grip as she rolls and bucks beneath me until a shudder wracks her body and a keening wail fills the room.

But I know it's not over for her yet, so I keep going, taking my fill until she quiets. Her thighs are sweat-slicked and coated with her arousal, and I want nothing more than to cover my cock in all that sweet goodness, to sink into her soft flesh and bury myself to the hilt. Alison raises her head and gives me a shy smile that burrows straight into my chest. A knot forms deep behind my sternum as we gaze at each other. "Wow," she says, her smile reaching her eyes. "Just. Wow."

My chest puffs. I know I'm good, but to see Alison the ball buster, languid and clearly satisfied, fluffs my ego.

She bites her lower lip and turns her face away. "I... I should go get dressed."

I rise from the floor to stand over her, my cock jutting hard and heavy between us. "Oh hell, no, angel. We're just getting started."

Chapter Nine

Alison

*H*is cock is enormous. Seriously. Enormous. And beautiful. All I can do is stare- at the flared crown, deep and dark, nearly purple, at the pulsing vein along his shaft, at the thick length of it. My mouth waters to taste it, more, I want it inside me so bad, that I can feel the ache building in my cunt again. The sensation surprises me. I'm unprepared for the hot lick of desire lashing at my nipples and racing down to my clit. "W-we are?" I stammer, flicking my gaze to his, then back to his cock, and up to his eyes again. He's dead serious.

He glances at the old-fashioned clock on my bedside table, then looms over me, his cock coming to rest on my belly. "It's barely eight. What part of all night didn't you understand?"

My body thrills at his declaration even as I wonder if I can possibly last that long. "What did you have in mind?"

His gaze sharpens, and the corner of his mouth curls

up as if he has all manner of dirty activities in mind. "Grab my cock," he orders with an edge to his voice that sends tingles of awareness rushing through my body.

I reach between us to grab it and as soon as I wrap my hand around its girth, I know I never want to stop touching it. The skin is like the smoothest, softest velvet, although there's nothing soft underneath it. He's hard as iron, and I give a tentative stroke along his length, up to the engorged head, covered in beads of pre-come. My pussy throbs, when he lets out a guttural noise, desperately wanting in on the action. It would be so easy to shimmy up the bed, and guide him into me, to let this beautiful instrument fill me up. My dildos will pale in comparison after this.

Condoms, the last shred of rationality reminds me harshly.

But I'm on the pill...

Nico Case isn't exactly trustworthy, my brain points out.

True. I should listen to the protective part of me, the part that got me out of a toxic marriage, the part that works to build me up and keep me emotionally safe. Yet, in this? I feel like I can trust Nico. I shouldn't, but I do.

He drops his head, bringing his mouth to mine, gently pumping into my hand, while his tongue slides along mine. I taste myself, a mildly salty, round addition to the sharp flavor of him I've quickly come to enjoy. He breaks our kiss only for a moment. "This is how I'm going to fuck you once we get those condoms."

"What if I want it harder?" I challenge, because I can't resist.

"Oh you'll get it that way, too," he promises darkly. "But right now, I want to fuck those gorgeous tits of yours."

I'm all in. Too late, I think of the stretch marks. "Can we turn off the light?"

"Fuck, no," he grits. "No hiding."

That's all I want to do- hide. And the fact that he said 'no hiding' means he knows exactly why I would want the lights off. Suddenly, this all feels too big, too scary. Too dangerous- like I've been cracked open and my soft under-belly has been exposed. A lobster without her shell. I have so much more confidence in the dark. My gaze snaps to his. All I see there is heat. Unabashed lust.

"What are you afraid of, Alison?" He asks with a sand-paper edge to his voice. "I've already seen all of you."

Humiliation.

Ridicule.

The words pop unbidden into my mind. But that's the old me talking, I remind myself harshly. I'm the new hotness, dammit. I deserve to have a satisfactory sex life with whatever partner I choose. I deserve to have orgasms. As many as I want- which let's face it, is all the damn time. And if someone as lickable as Nico Case wants to give them to me, why the fuck would I say no? I suppose I should thank Tommy for teaching me that when it comes to women like me, men aren't emotionally trustworthy. I will never again invest emotionally in another man, but that doesn't mean I have to be a nun. Nico is just the man to end my dry spell. I push the fear away and allow myself to relax. "You're right. Old habits, I guess." I pull his head down and kiss him, because if I kiss him enough, focus only on the physical, I can chase away the demons that haunt me

He quickly takes over, making hungry noises as he devours me. The heat builds between my legs. He licks down my neck to the valley between my breasts, teasing my nipples. No one's ever played with my tits this way, and I fucking love it. Apparently there's a direct line between my nips and my clit, and the more he bites and pulls and licks, the stronger the throbbing becomes until I'm writhing beneath him, searching for friction, anything to soothe the needy ache.

He climbs over me, his cock pushing across my belly until it rests between my breasts. I'm surprised at how much I like it, and for once, I'm not ashamed of my double D's. I push my boobs together, and he strokes through. "Yeah," he grunts. "That's hot."

It is. And I'm just as turned on as he is. I squeeze my thighs together, because I'm desperate for some kind of touch on my clit. He curses when I lift my head to lick the engorged head as his cock peeks out from between my breasts. I do it again, this time, taking him into my mouth as he thrusts forward. The sharp masculine taste of him fills my senses and we groan together. I feel a surge of power that's as arousing as his cock in my mouth. It's intoxicating, the knowledge that Nico Case, my one-time tormentor, is trembling with the need to release, and that *I* made him that way. His movements become jerky, erratic, as he nears his climax. I feel it the second he crashes over the edge. He pulls back, hard, and lets out a shout, coming all over my tits with hot spurts of come that cover my chest and throat. I'm so aroused, I squeeze my thighs in little pulses chasing my own orgasm.

He sits back on his heels, and I'm amazed to see his cock still full. I'm sure I go bug-eyed, because he lets out a low laugh. "I told you we're just getting started." He gives himself a stroke, and fuck if his cock doesn't firm up. "I can see your hot little cunt is ready for attention." I can only whimper when he pulls his cock over my sensitized clit. "Fuck, Alison, you're so wet." He rubs at me, and god help me, I want it. I want it filling me up. I rub shamelessly against him like a cat in heat. "Ahh, we shouldn't be doing this," he grunts, not stopping. "But you feel so fucking good."

All my sister Kimmie's warnings sound in my head. All the education about unprotected sex, about how men will say anything to get into your pants, but fuck if Nico doesn't make me want to take a walk on the wild side. I've never had unprotected sex. Tommy never trusted my birth control, and insisted we use condoms on the rare occasion we'd have sex. Looking back, that should have been a red-flag from the get-go. But I was young and dumb... and desperate. This time, my desperation only comes from a need to release. And it's turned me into a depraved lunatic with only one goal. "I'm on the pill," I blurt.

Yep, I've lost my mind.

But ask me if I care, because I'm burning up with lust.

Above me, Nico freezes.

"I'm clean and haven't had a partner in two years."

"Two years?" comes his strangled reply.

My face burns, but before I can lose myself in a sea of shame, he shakes his head with a laugh that borders on rueful. "It's been nearly a year for me."

"But you're-"

"Married. Was. But we can wait until we have condoms," he offers, still stroking my clit with his cock and making it difficult to speak, let alone think.

My chest grows tight. Nico Case is an asshole, a taker. He doesn't have a thoughtful bone in his body. Against my will, his offer touches me. And simultaneously scares the shit out of me, because it would be all too easy to fall for a nicer version of Nico. I shake my head, pushing the thoughts into a deep dark corner of my psyche to examine later. "Fucking. *Now*," I growl, thrusting my hips.

At the same time, he pushes into me with a guttural

moan. "Jeezus," he grits through a clenched jaw. "You're so fucking tight. So hot."

I am the new hotness, I remind myself as he pushes deeper inside me, filling me up, stretching me until I think I might split. "You're. So. Big," I gasp in between breaths. I'm an addict. There is no way I will ever get enough of this sensation, his weight pressing me into the bed, his rock hard ass underneath my hands, as he goes deeper with each thrust.

He drops his head, kissing the hollow between my neck and my collarbone. "I'm going to fuck you slowly, angel," he says thrusting into the heart of me, then slowly pulling out and stroking my clit in the process.

I'm practically there, and it only takes a few strokes before my orgasm builds to bursting, and crashes over me in a cascade of rainbow sparkles behind my eyes. But he doesn't stop, he keeps up his slow and steady pace, through each wave of nerve numbing tingles. Then, he does something entirely unexpected. He pulls my thighs wider, and slips his hands beneath my ass, squeezing. "Lift your hips," he orders.

I obey, and nearly see stars. The angle hits the deepest part of me, and an uncontrollable ache builds somewhere deep in my belly as he thrusts harder, faster. I feel like I'm falling, like I'm going to break apart, explode into little atoms. I cry out, words incoherent. I'm flying, I'm crashing. I register his voice joining mine, his fingers squeezing into my ass hard enough to leave marks, but I feel no pain, only white light emanating from my womb. And when the second orgasm hits with the ferocity of a runaway train, I shout, losing myself in a tidal wave of ecstasy.

Chapter Ten

Nico

I collapse onto Alison, utterly spent. We both must have dozed, because the clock shows eleven p.m. when I glance over to her bedside table. I kiss her temple, and her eyes flutter open. I like her this way, soft-eyed, full mouth curved into a smile, body soft beneath me. I could get dangerously used to this. I push the thought from my head. Alison doesn't even like me, and she's *way* to bossy for me. Still... I can't help but wonder what she's like underneath the hard exterior she's clearly erected around herself.

"Shower?"

She nods. "You go first."

I push up onto my elbows. "Hell, no. You're coming with me."

Panic flits across her face. "I-I don't think it's a good idea."

"Clearly, you've never had shower sex."

"Shower sex?" she repeats. "Is that even a thing?"

I nod.

"But- logistics," she protests. "I'm five-two. I'm pretty sure we don't line up."

"Creativity trumps logistics," I say with a dark chuckle. I see desire flicker in her eyes, warring with indecision. A knot in my chest loosens when I see desire win out. "You want me to show you?"

She gives a shy nod, and awareness shoots through me. Maybe it's because I haven't been laid in too damned long, but I can't get enough of her. My cock thickens where it rests between her thighs.

"C'mon." I push off the bed, not missing the way her eyebrows shoot skyward when she catches sight of my cock bobbing, hungry for more. I offer my hand, and she accepts my help off the bed. I pull her into the bathroom and turn on the faucet. The shower couldn't be more perfect for two people. Not only is the shower head one of those large, fancy rain shower discs, ensuring enough stream for the both of us, there's a built-in bench at the far end, which currently holds a myriad of shampoos and body washes, but will be perfect for other, more dirty uses. But first things first. I pull her into the hot water, and take a minute to soap up a washcloth. I rub her from head to toe, paying extra attention to the places I've discovered drive her wild. In moments, she's panting and flushed, pupils so wide her eyes are black. Her enthusiasm only eggs me on.

It's been ages, since before I married Veronica- since before she lost our child, that sex has been an adventure in pleasure. I've often wondered if Ronnie set me up from the beginning. I was obsessed with hitting my older brother Jason where I thought he was most vulnerable. Yet ever since the ink dried on the divorce papers, I can't help but think Ronnie's end game was our family's fortune, however she could get it, and I was too hellbent on revenge to see the signs. Never again.

"Turn around," I say roughly. "Hands on the bench."

She complies, then looks over her shoulder. "Like this?"

Oh fuck, yes. Her pussy, crimson and swollen, peeks out from between her plump ass cheeks. "Spread your legs wider." I reach forward to graze a finger over her heated flesh. It comes away coated in her sex. She wiggles her ass with a whimper. "You want more?" I ask, finding her clit. She's slippery with arousal, and makes a pleading noise in her throat. I find her entrance, and push in with a finger, stroking her g-spot until she cries out, clenching her walls around my finger. "You want my cock in here, sweetheart? Filling up your cunt?" She nods vigorously, hips rolling like a fucking exotic dancer. Water runs in rivulets down her back, and I'm overcome with the need to mark her with my seed, to see my come run off her the same way the water does. I remove my finger, and grab her hips, thrusting into her in one quick, hard movement. Something unspools in my chest as soon as I'm fully seated in her tight heat. I wrap a hand around her waist, seeking and finding her clit, hard and slippery, and I begin to pump, first deep hard thrusts, then quick movements, changing it up as soon as she finds a rhythm. She pushes back into me with a moan of frustration and I slow, focusing on teasing her clit. I spread my legs, bracing myself against the sides of the shower, and bending so I cover her, so her heat becomes my heat. I stroke and thrust paying attention to every sound Alison makes, every catch of her breath, and soon, I can tell she's close. "Are you close?" I want to make sure.

"So close," she says tightly.

I drop my head and bite along her shoulder. She

squeals, then comes with a shudder, bearing down on my cock, the contractions of her channel rippling over my cock. I nearly spill myself, but she hasn't stopped shuddering, and I want to milk this from her, give her every last drop of pleasure. Fire licks up the back of my legs, tension spooling at the base of my spine, drawing my balls tight, coiling for release. I feel it coming, and pull out, letting go with a harsh cry and lashing her back in thick, white spurts of come. It's a beautiful sight, Alison's lower back and ass covered with my seed.

She looks back over her shoulder with a satisfied grin. "You're a dirty asshole," she says with a giggle that's so adorable, I want to take her again, right here in the shower. But we're running out of hot water, and I want to clean her off again. Only it doesn't quite go as I planned. We linger in the shower until it freezes us out, then we tumble out with a laugh. She grabs a towel and takes my hand, leading me back to the bedroom, where she spreads the towel on the bed. "I'm not done yet," she says, with a mischievous glint in her dark eyes.

"Oh?" Her tone of voice has my cock swelling even though I just fucked her silly.

She pushes me to sit on the edge of the bed, and drops her head, sliding her tongue across my shoulder, and down across my pec to nip at my nipple. An electric jolt goes straight to my balls. She nips again, and my cock bobs, thick and hard now. Her mouth keeps going lower, tracing my abs with her tongue, and teasing around the head of my cock when she reaches it.

"Jeezus, you don't know what you do to me," I groan. "Your mouth is the hottest fucking thing."

"I thought you said my cunt was," she giggles, breath skating over me, sensitizing my skin.

She takes me fully into her mouth, tongue lapping at

my shaft as my crown bumps the back of her throat. My eyes roll into the back of my head when she swallows. All I can do is make incoherent sounds and run my fingers through her silky dark hair. I want this to go on forever, and it's only with superhuman effort, I gently pull her off my cock. Tonight is about giving her all the orgasms, but I'm already thinking about when and where we can do this again, because *fuck*. Her eyes fill with confusion. "What? Was I bad?"

"Fuck, no." I grit, and scoot farther back on the bed, pulling her on top of me. "Your mouth, *and* your cunt are fucking incredible. But I want a taste of these."

I palm her breast, loving how the flesh spills out of my hand, and a draw a nipple into my mouth, tonguing it into a hard peak, pulling and licking at it, while she slides her slick pussy back and forth along my cock. "I really like that," she admits shyly, and again I'm struck by the funny feeling in my chest her words create.

"Do you like this, too?" I ask, adjusting her hips so that she slides onto my cock. It's sweet relief to be engulfed in her tight heat. She nods, mouth forming into an O. "Ride me however you want, angel." And fuck if she doesn't take me at my word. She rocks and rolls, tits bouncing gently as she takes me fully. It's a beautiful sight, her luscious curvy body pink from our shower and from her arousal, her dark areolas puckering around hard nubs. I take one into my mouth, pleasuring her however I can. My blood runs heavy and slow, thick with craving for this woman. Only fucking will slake the deep need she's triggered inside me. Only seeing her repeatedly come apart will satisfy my craven thirst for her. And come apart she does, like an asteroid burning a path across the night sky, flaring brightly, breaking into pieces and floating down to meet the ground. She contracts around me, milking me dry as I follow her into the abyss. My mind goes blank as I drive into her, emptying every last drop of come into her womb.

She collapses against me with a deep, satisfied sigh, and I'm struck with the realization that I could stay like this all night- legs tangled, bodies slick with sweat, in the barely conscious haze that invariably comes with mind-blowing orgasms. Which means, I need to force myself up and out of here. Right now. Alison raises her head, a bemused smile flickering at the corner of her mouth. We speak at the same time.

"I should go."

"You need to go."

What? I'm the one who's supposed to make that call. I'm the one in charge here. I stare at her, dumbfounded.

"I mean it," she reiterates. "It's time for you to go."

"To the couch?"

Her smile spreads, making her eyes crinkle. "Unless you have some other place you're planning on sleeping."

"Yeah. Right here." I don't like being dismissed like this, and I wonder briefly if this is how it felt to the myriad of girls I sent home with a 'see you around' and a pat on the ass in the years before I hooked up with Veronica.

Her mouth quirks, and she shakes her head with a breathy laugh. "Nope. Sorry, I need my beauty sleep and that means going to bed alone."

"But it's the middle of the night," I protest. I can't believe I'm arguing. I should get up and strut down the hall, showing her what she's going to be missing by kicking me out.

"All the more reason." She pushes herself up and off the bed, gliding to the bathroom, ass swaying as if kicking me out is the most natural thing in the world. "Do you need anything?" she calls from the bathroom over the sound of the faucet. "A toothbrush? An extra blanket?"

No. I need her back in bed, soft body curled into mine. But I know when to concede defeat, and I've definitely lost this battle. I rise and stalk to the bathroom, coming to stand behind her. She catches my eye in the mirror, and watches captivated as I trail fingers down her spine. In the mirror, I see her nipples rise and harden. A shiver ripples down her back, and I bring my mouth to the sensitive spot where her neck melts into her shoulder. Her breath hitches, and I glance to the mirror again, her teeth have clamped down on that beautifully plump lower lip. "Good night, angel."

My cock is thick and hard when I step away, and I pause long enough for her to catch a glimpse in the mirror of what she's missing. "Sweet dreams," I say with a laugh as I turn and head for the couch.

Chapter Eleven

Alison

I wake up late. And pleasantly sore. The kind of sore that makes me stretch like a satisfied cat, and regret kicking Nico out of my bed in the middle of the night. Almost... because if he was naked in bed next to me... I roll over with a sigh. There's too much work to be done today, and the crew will be here in less than an hour.

I rise and get dressed. My nipples ache, and I've got bruises across the tops of my breasts and along the inside of my thighs where Nico feasted on my flesh. Maybe it's juvenile, and certainly depraved, but I like wearing the reminder of our no-holds-barred sexcapades. I want more. The temptation to march down the hall and climb on top of him is real. But this can't happen again. Ever. Declan would fire me for starters, and no matter how Nico might hint that he's different, somehow. I know he's not. I mean, Jeezus, the guy knocked up his brother's fiancé, then married her. Who does that kind of shit?

Assholes.

Degenerates.

Surely not nice guys who wouldn't mind settling down someday with a chubby half Asian girl with brains too big for her skull, and a mouth that doesn't know when to stop.

I step into the hall, shutting the door quietly behind me. Nico's snores echo down the hall, and a delightfully evil idea enters my mind. I should record him and use the footage for leverage. You never know when something like that would come in handy, especially given the kind of guy Nico Case is. But I can't bring myself to take advantage like that. Especially when I spot that he's cleared the table, cleaned up the kitchen, *and* put last night's unfinished meal in the fridge. Who does *that?* Definitely not assholes. It makes me uneasy when he ventures into nice-guy territory, when he does things that make him... likable.

He's just being a polite house-guest, I remind myself sternly. On the whole, the Case brothers are a self-interested lot, with no altruistic bones in any of their bodies, and I can't afford to forget that for even a second. In fact, I need to be as self-interested as they are. Declan Case handed me the opportunity of a lifetime, and I need to capitalize the shit out of that. By my calculations, I should be able to buy him out in six years, five if I get lucky.

I slip outside and cross the yard to my favorite spot, my unease dissipating as I take in the view. I need to stay focused on my goals, on my future. I pull out my phone and dial my sister. "I've been thinking about you all day today," Kimmie says with a note of concern in her voice when she answers. "Is everything okay?"

My older sister has always been psychic like that. Ever since I was a baby. She's told me since we were little that we're cosmically attached- she asked her parents for a baby sister for her sixth birthday, and damn if I wasn't born *on* her birthday. And she's been the best- she's never judged me, and she has every reason to- for starters she's as tall and slender as I am short and wide. She's perfectly poised, and naturally, perfectly beautiful. And if that's not enough, she's also wildly successful- the Vice-President of branding for one of Seoul's top cosmetics companies. There's no competing with her because she's perfect. She always has been, but not in an awful way, because she's also the kindest, most generous, most caring person I know. And she's been there for me through all of the high-school garbage, the moving away and changing my name, the lap band surgery after my divorce- everything. I love her with a fierce devotion that's only matched by my parents.

"It could be, I suppose," not quite sure how to broach the subject.

"Hmmm. I'm not encouraged by that. Is it the vineyard? Are you *sure* it's a good idea working for one of the Case triplets? I worry..." Her voice trails off.

"I know, and yes, the vineyard's going great. *And* I discovered these abandoned barrels in the cellar that are phenomenal. Declan's given me the go-ahead to name them, and market the shit out of them." That's not why I called, but I'm stalling. As much as she has my back, she's going to flip when I tell her I spent the night fucking Nico.

I can hear the smile in her voice. "That's fantastic. I'm *so* proud of you, Bean."

I warm at the old nickname. She started calling me that when mom was pregnant with me, and it stuck. And even though the elementary kids started calling me Soybean when they heard Kimmie call me Bean, it never hurt in the deep soul-marring way the other insults did when I got fat in the fifth grade.

"Thanks, sis. I *know* this is going to put Fieldstone Winery on the map."

"So you've finally come up with a name for the vineyard? I love it," she enthuses. One thing I adore about Kimmie is her infectious enthusiasm. It's why she's good at her job- she falls in love with every new product her company develops.

"Thought about it yesterday while I was pruning with-while I was pruning." I catch myself too late, and Kimmie is too attentive to miss it.

"With who?"

I take a deep breath. "Nicholas Case," I say with my heart pounding up around my throat.

"What?" she asks, voice dropping two-hundred degrees to absolute zero. In that moment, she sounds like our grandma who used to scare the shit out of us when we were little kids and my parents would leave us with her to go on an occasional date. "Tell me you didn't just say what I thought you said."

My face heats. I feel like I'm having a hot flash as my insides burn up. "I did," I say in a small voice, suddenly feeling about eight-years-old again.

"Are you *insane*, Bean? Swift death is too good for him. You know, I have connections…"

I totally believe it. She travels in some crazy circles in Seoul. "But it's-"

"He needs to be staked out in the desert and fed to the ants," she says with absolute disgust in her voice. Gotta love fierce sister love.

I pull in another deep breath, gathering my courage. "He's not like that anymore, sis. He's… different."

She scoffs. "Leopards never change their spots."

"No, really. You'd see, if you were here. Andhe'ssuper-hotandImighthavefuckedhimlastnight," I finish in a rush.

My confession is met with silence. For a moment, I wonder if she's hung up. Or thrown her phone across the room. "You might have fucked him," she says after several more strained moments of silence. "*ARE YOU FUCKING KIDDING ME?*" she screeches, and I have to pull the phone from my ear. My whole body burns with shame. I hate it when Kimmie gets mad at me. It's maybe only happened a handful of times in our lives, and most of the time it comes from a place of righteous indignation on my behalf, but it still makes my stomach fill with bile and my body burn with the worst kind of desperate self-loathing.

I bite a nail, second-guessing the call. I should have been prepared for this.

"*Katie,*" she reprimands. "Honey, you deserve so much better than the likes of him."

"Don't call me that," I murmur, tears springing to my eyes. "Katie's gone."

"You'll *always* be my Katie-bug, little Bean," she says with such deep mourning that a tear sneaks out of my eye.

And another follows behind it, dammit. "I can't *be* that anymore. You know that."

She sniffs dramatically. "I know, I know, but sweetie, you're playing with fire. This won't end well. He's bound to find out. You can't keep something like that buried forever."

"Tommy never knew."

"Tommy never deserved to know," she spits.

"Neither does Nico. And I'm never going to tell him. Look, it was just a thing," I add after a pause. "A blip, a chemical explosion."

"Well it better have been the best fucking sex you've ever had, then."

"Oh it was."

"Ohmygod." She lets out a half-hysterical laugh. "I'm just having a hard time wrapping my head around this. I suppose as long as you know what you're doing…"

"I have no idea what I'm doing," I admit.

"You have to admit, the irony is something else."

I nod. "Yeah," I wonder if he'd look at me differently, knowing I was Katie the Cow. I don't want to find out.

"You should make him fall in love with you, then dump his ass," she says spitefully.

"Kimmie," I gasp, scandalized. "You know I'm not that vindictive."

"But I am," she says, deadly serious. And this is why I absolutely adore my sister. She would go to the mat for me, or worse. There was a moment during my divorce when she threatened to rip Tommy's balls off. I think he believed she would, because he was much more cooperative after that. "And you should be," she adds. "God knows, he deserves all your wrath and then some."

"Can we change the subject? Please?" I plead. "I've tried my best to move beyond all that crap."

"Fine. Just promise me you won't fuck him again."

A knot presses into the spot just beneath my sternum. I've never broken a promise to my sister. I'm sorely tempted to say no... because holy hell, I want a repeat of last night more than anything. But she's looking out for me, and she's right- Nico Case is dangerous business. I nod with more than a little regret. "I won't."

"Promise me."

"I promise."

Chapter Twelve

Nico

*I*t's mid-afternoon, and Alison has been coolly professional since she came in from her morning walk. Surprisingly cool given the heat we generated last night.

"You need to start fertilizing." I know I'm poking the bear, but I can't help it. I'm tired of being ignored, and I'm not a complete idiot when it comes to winemaking.

My comment doesn't even earn me a sideways glance. She keeps thinning the grapes like I commented on the weather. "You need to stop acting like you know what you're doing."

"I'm just looking out for my brother."

"I am too." She opens her mouth to say more, but then snaps it shut with a shake of her head. "Fine. You don't trust me? Vet me. Call Danny Pendergast. I assume you know Danny?"

I do. Danny Pendergast is one of Dec's best friends

from our time at Stanford. In addition to being the great-grandson of a notorious Kansas City gangster, he's built a whiskey club that's sought after by the most influential wheelers and dealers in the country, some of them with less than... pure connections. You want to buy a company, make a real-estate deal, procure rare art, anything- you go to Danny. "How do you know Danny?"

"Doesn't matter. Danny recommended me for the job."

I deflate. If Danny recommended her to Dec, then she's the real deal. Danny only surrounds himself with the best. But if that's the case, how come I've never heard of her? I might not be on a first-name basis with the top guys in Napa, but we at least know each other by sight. "Is that so? Then how come I've never seen your name in print?"

I can feel the righteous anger bristling off her. "Practical Winery and Vineyard. Last year's-" She stops and throws up her hands. "Why am I justifying myself? I don't need to justify myself to you." Her voice takes an icy edge. "You have a problem with me? Talk to Declan. Hell, call Danny. I have work to do today." She turns on her heel and marches away, only to stop and march back, jabbing a finger into my chest. "Contrary to what you might think, Napa is not the center of the wine universe. Try reading something beyond the Napa Wine Examiner."

"Look, sweetheart. I-"

"And another thing," she interrupts gesticulating wildly. "We are not repeating last night. Ever."

"Damn straight," I drawl. "I don't make a habit of bedding bossy mouths." Only my cock is fired up from all this arguing, and I'd like nothing better than to tumble her into the grass and discover if she tastes as delicious *al fresco*.

"*Bossy mouth?*" Her outraged gasp is of comic book proportions, and I bite the inside of my cheek to keep from laughing. "Bossy mouth? You haven't even *begun* to see bossy mouth."

Weaker men would wither under the glare she aims at me, but all I want to do is poke at her some more, wind her up, and then kiss her senseless. "I think I need a lobotomy," I mutter under my breath.

"Oh you need more than that," she snaps back.

I step into her space, close enough that her breath skates across my collarbone. I duck my head and murmur into her ear. "Nice to know your hearing is as sharp as your tongue. *Bossy mouth,*" I add with a low chuckle.

Her gaze snaps to mine and the air between us sizzles. I still, a current of awareness sensitizing my nerve endings. Her eyelids flutter and her mouth softens. The urge to lean in and kiss her is powerful. I want to taste what she's like all fired-up, feel her hard shell soften beneath my fingers, obey the demands of my tongue.

Energy coils low in my belly, ready to release, but I don't get my chance, because I hear Carla, hollering from the top of the hill. Alison steps back, but not before I see her shoulders vibrate with a shiver. "I-I've got to take care of some things in the crushing pad. You know what to do here, and Carla can answer any questions you have."

She steps back, and turns, jogging up the hill. I whip out my phone. I don't care that it's Sunday afternoon, I'm fucking calling Danny. He answers on the third ring. "Let me guess," he drawls. "You've met Alison."

Danny also has an uncanny, almost psychic ability to foresee trouble- long before it actually arises. I'd bet what little money is left in my bank account that he's been waiting for my call. I cut to the chase. "She said you recommended her to Dec."

"Indeed I did."

"So she's legit." I make it more of a statement than a question.

"Are you implying I'd purposefully screw over Declan?"

He would if it meant saving his own ass, and we both know that. "What's her story?"

He chuckles. "What makes you think there's a story?"

"There's *always* a story," I remind him. Danny makes a point of knowing all of his associates' stories. He considers it insurance.

"She has a double degree from Cornell- microbiology and enology, *summa cum laude.* She interned in France and Spain under two winemakers I personally know and respect, and she's been an assistant winemaker at a vine- yard just outside of Kansas City."

"Why not head?"

"No one's given her a shot." I can sense Danny's irrita- tion, but he's gonna have to suck it up and answer my damn questions.

"Family?"

"Dad's from Seoul, is president of a pharmaceutical company on the Kansas side. Mom's from good Midwestern stock. Sister is VP of Brand Awareness for a cosmetics company in Seoul. Anything else?"

"Yeah. How do *you* know her?"

Danny's voice turns cold. "Privileged information."

"Not if she's working for my brother it's not."

"Oh hell, yes it is. I've answered your questions. She's legit, she's talented, she's smarter than you *and* your brothers put together, and if you stay the hell out of her way, she'll make Declan a fuck-ton of money. *Capisci?*"

Funny, hearing a descendant of an Irish mobster use Italian. But I get the message, loud and clear. "Yeah, yeah."

"And another thing. Keep it zipped around her. Get what I mean? She's too good for the likes of you."

On that point, we agree. And while I sure as hell am not gonna 'fess up that we've already dallied in the garden of earthly delights, I'm also not going there again, no matter how hard my dick begs. No way, no how. Miss Bossy Mouth is going firmly in the one-night-stand column.

Chapter Thirteen

Nico

*A*lison struts down the hall looking like a million damned bucks. I let out a low whistle. "Where are you going?" It's clear she's off to somewhere. She's wearing hot pink leather ankle boots that I want wrapped around my neck while I devour her. Her hair falls in soft waves behind her shoulders, and she's wearing fuck-me-pink lipstick that matches her boots. She's wearing a tunic similar to the one I ripped off of her last night- only this time in a deep shade of turquoise that sets off her skin and her eyes perfectly. I want to rip it off her all over again. And then I'm struck with the worst thought- *what if she's going on a date?*

The acrid taste of jealousy rises in my throat. Surely, she's not that cold? I mean, I know it was just one night, and I have zero claim to her whatsoever, but it doesn't stop an ugly taste from creeping into my mouth.

"Out," she says, gently placing four wine bottles

labeled with masking tape into a thermal carrier. "Don't expect me for dinner. Help yourself to the leftovers."

"Where are you going?" I ask again. I know it's none of my damned business, except… I want to know.

She narrows her eyes and stares at me. When she speaks, her voice is laced with suspicion. "Why do you want to know?"

I close the distance between us and brace my arms on the counter, not breaking eye-contact. "Because maybe I'm a little concerned about your safety," I state in clipped words with more than a little steel in my voice.

Her eyes widen slightly, as if she's surprised by my answer. But then she rolls her eyes with a wave of her hand. "No need to worry about me. I can take care of myself."

"I will absodamnlutely worry about your sweet little ass when it's out of my sight, angel." The strength of my vehemence shocks me. But it's true.

She chuckles with a shake of her head, then stares me down. "You got one thing wrong, pretty boy. There's nothing little about my ass. And thank you very much, but I can take care of myself."

"Can you?"

She glares. "Of course I can."

"I have no doubt of your overconfidence in order to prove a point."

"And I have no doubt of your fake concern," she snaps.

I stalk around the counter, right into her space, close enough I catch a whiff of her rose-scented lotion and a layer of enticing floral perfume. Her mouth drops open in surprise. I want to kiss her, smudge her pretty pink lipstick. "Let's get one thing straight, sweetheart. I don't fucking lie." Not anymore.

Pain flares briefly in her eyes. "Ha."

"You don't have to believe me, but it's the truth. Now tell me, *where the fuck are you going?*"

She lets out a big sigh and rolls her eyes. "I'm going to the Napa Winemaker's mixer. No need to worry at all."

"I'm going with you."

Her eyes snap to mine. "What?" She shakes her head. "Oh hell no. I did not sign up for this shit."

"You afraid I'm going to steal your thunder?"

Her mouth thins, and I bite my cheek, because laughing right now might cost me my balls. "No. I'm afraid you're going to be an enormous pain in my ass."

I step back and open my hands. "I can't promise I won't. But I do promise to be on my best behavior. And I'm coming with you."

She stares at me a long second, jaw set. The conflict flickers on her face. "Fine. But you aren't saying a word, got it?"

"It'll be like I'm not even there," I promise, stupidly delighted she's given an inch. I head to the closet and shove an arm into my jacket. "We can take my bike."

"No way." She grabs her keys from the dish at the edge of the counter. "I'm driving."

"What is it, angel?" I grin broadly. "Afraid of being too close to me?"

"Of course not," she denies too quickly.

"So you're afraid of motorcycles."

"Absolutely not," she says, brimming with exasperation.

"So you have no problem riding behind me then. I can strap the wine to the back."

She scowls. "Okay, fine. Let me get my jacket." She stomps past me to her bedroom and emerges a moment later wearing a leather motorcycle jacket. It's hot as fuck, half-zipped and nipping in at her waist. I want to see her in that and nothing else but those fuck-me-pink booties.

"You're something else, Ali."

She ignores my compliment and stalks to the door. "Let's go."

I love riding my bike. I love the feeling of leaving my problems behind, of the possibility that lies around the next corner, the feel of the wind, the sense that you can reach out your hand and touch the trees. But nothing compares to having Alison behind me on the bike, thighs glued to mine, chest pressed against me and holding on for dear life. I'm engulfed in her embrace, her essence, and I swear, I can feel her heart beating through the layers of leather.

Chapter Fourteen

Nico

$\mathcal{T}$he forty-minute drive to the bar on the outskirts of Yountville where the monthly meeting takes place goes too fast, and I hate the loss of her body when she slides off the bike. She pauses at the door, worrying her lower lip.

"What is it?" I ask gruffly, stomach sinking as I prepare for her request.

"So… inside…"

"Yes?" I prompt. I've already noticed that when she's nervous, she doesn't cut to the chase the way she does the rest of the time. She toes a rock with the tip of her boots. "Let me guess," I fill in. "You want me to make myself scarce."

My voice must convey my disappointment, because her eyes snap to mine. "It's not like we're on a date. We're not even partners," she adds defensively.

I open my hands. "Don't worry, sweetheart, I'll make

myself scarce." I get it, I do. She wants to make her mark, all on her own. But part of me hates her blanket rejection. I pull open the door and wave her in. "Holler if you need anything."

She nods and passes, and I make no attempt to hide the fact that I'm staring at her ass the whole way in. There's so much I'd love to do with that ass, with all of her, and I have to sternly remind myself that I've firmly placed her in the one-night stand column.

She pauses at the table to fill out a name tag, and hands over the bag with the wine. I haven't been to one of these since before all my family drama. I only started going because Ronnie started dragging me to these sometime last year. I should have suspected then that something was up, but once again, I was too self-absorbed to read the clues. I fill out my name tag and brace myself for a handful of awkward conversations.

"Can I get a picture of you two?" A young woman I've never seen before asks as we leave the table.

"With him?" Alison asks, giving me a skeptical glance.

"Sure," I grin, slipping my arm around her waist and pulling her into my side. "You bet."

"I'm Brittany, the communications intern for the wine-maker's association. Can you tell me your names?"

"I'm Alison Walker, winemaker at Fieldstone Wineries on Mt. Veeder, and this is Nicholas Case." On the outside, she's all smiles, but I can feel the tension running through her body.

Brittany's eyes go wide. "As in Case Family Wineries?"

I'd be rich if I got a nickel every time someone asked that. "Indeed."

Brittany whips out a notebook. "So is Fieldstone Wineries a new Case venture?"

"No," Alison says forcefully. "Not at all."

"Oh, do you own the vineyard, then?"

Alison tenses, but keeps her smile in place. "I'm just the winemaker."

Just the winemaker, my ass. I've only been there a short time, but already I can see she's a helluva lot more than 'just the winemaker.'

"So who's the owner then?"

She gives me another sidelong glance, jaw ticking. "Declan Case," she says quietly.

"So it *is* a Case venture?" Brittany says excitedly. "Do I have permission to scoop this? This is big news. I'd love to help create some buzz for you."

I can sense Alison deflating, and I take a breath to say something, but she squeezes my forearm, hard. "Sure. Be my guest," she answers with a wry smile. "It was bound to get out sooner or later."

Brittany bounces on her toes. "My boss will be so excited. Can I call you for an in-depth interview later?"

"Of course." Alison makes her excuses and slips out of my embrace, disappearing to the other side of the room.

Pride swells in my chest as I watch her stop and speak with another winemaker. Alison is the picture of graciousness- not only to the young intern, but to everyone she encounters - a trait Ronnie never bothered to perfect. I shouldn't compare the two, but it's hard not to. For the most part, the crowd is friendly. The first part of the evening is always meet and greet, then after, any winemaker who wants, can step up and pour samples. It's supposed to be a supportive environment where winemakers can do a little bragging about a reserve, or get opinions on whether or not a wine is ready to release. But Napa isn't without its competitive sharks, and there are enough of those types here tonight, I worry that Alison might be their chum.

"So glad to see you haven't gone into permanent hiding, Case," a familiar voice comments while a hand slaps my back. My skin crawls. Kevin Martin is an asshat of epic proportions. I'm pretty sure he spent every one of these meetings trying to crawl into Ronnie's panties. He's a talented winemaker, but I'd never work for him, or let anyone else I know work for him.

I extend my hand while stepping back, creating distance. "Nice to see you, Kevin, how've you been?"

Kevin eyes me. He's an opportunistic fuck, and my guess is that right now he's trying to decide if it's in his best interests to butter me up or to give me the cold shoulder. "Fine, fine. Say… what can you tell me about the fat chick you came in with?"

I grind my teeth, fisting my hand at my side. But with Kevin, it's always best to stay cool. He's got a nasty habit of pushing people to the breaking point, then somehow coming out squeaky clean. He's not going to best me today. "You mean the winemaker? Alison Walker?" My eyes land on her, and I bite my tongue to not give away anything. I lift a shoulder, doing my best to look bored. "Don't know anything about her." Except that I fucking love her pussy, and the way she cries out my name when she's coming all over my cock.

Kevin's eyes narrow. "That so? I heard she was working for your brother."

News travels fast, and gossip travels faster. It's no secret she's working for Declan, and I'm guessing the info came from one of the staff members at Central Valley. "Yeah, she is," I acknowledge.

"What's her background?"

I smirk. "Sizing up the competition?"

Kevin scowls. "It's just that nobody's heard of her."

"And your point is?" I know what his point is. There's a

small cadre of winemakers, led by Kevin and a few others, who believe that Napa's being polluted with highly stylized wines marketed to millennials.

He lowers his voice. "You know. We just want to keep Napa's winemaking practices pure. You know, Napa for Napa."

Fuck him. I clap him on the back with a smile that doesn't reach my eyes. "Did anyone tell you that you win the award for being Napa's biggest douchebag? If not, let me congratulate you."

His facial expression as what I've said sinks in, is worth burning the bridge, and there's no doubt I've burned a bridge, but I don't give a shit. "You…you…" he sputters, mouth moving but no sound coming out.

I lean in, so only he can hear. "And let's get one thing straight, asshole. If I hear any shit circulating about Alison, I'll burn your goddamn vineyard down. That's a promise." And I'll get Danny to help me. I give him one last smile and move away, feeling immensely satisfied.

I scan the room and find Alison talking with another woman, older- maybe mid-forties. She's easily the youngest here by a good ten years. As I make my way through the room, another person catches my arm. "So the prince has lost his crown," a feminine voice says with an edge meant to cut. "What makes you think you'll find it here among the poor masses?"

I turn, smiling grimly. "Hello, Susan. Nice to see you again." Susan Hughes works for one of our competitors, because when Dad bought the vineyard she was working at, he fired her. What she doesn't know, was that it was me who suggested it. Maybe she's figured it out, or maybe she's hated us ever since. Either way, there's no love lost here.

She glares at me, green eyes glittering with icy shards.

"Why are you here, Nico? Come to scout another acquisition?"

"Nope, just here to enjoy a little company and conversation." And look after Alison.

"Good luck with that."

"Nice to see you, Susan," I say, forcing myself to remain polite. Nobody loves dog piling more than a group of people with a bone to pick, and as I survey the room, I can guess that a good chunk of these guys have a bone to pick with me, one way or another.

I scan for Alison again and see she's moved to another group of men. I'm instantly on alert because one fucker keeps stealing looks at her chest. I watch with half fascination and half possessive jealousy. She angles her body away from the guy and keeps chatting with two others. But when he puts his hand on the small of her back, my feet propel me forward. I wonder how fast I'd get blacklisted if I rearranged his face? Hell, from the sneers and sideways glances I'm getting from half the room, I'm probably already blacklisted. Fuck 'em. Only polite while they know you have money and influence. *Only polite because they have to be, 'cause they think you're an asshole,* the dark voice inside my conscience reminds me. I deflate a little at the thought.

I join their group with a smile. "I see you've met my brother's winemaker." I can feel the temperature cool twenty degrees. Alison shoots me a glare and gives a subtle shake of her head, but I'm all in and coming to her rescue. "Has she told you about the wine she discovered in the cellar? She brought some to taste tonight."

"But it's not yours," a guy I don't know clarifies.

Alison opens her mouth, but I beat her to it, in full CEO mode. "She didn't make it, but it's indicative of how the grapes perform, and we're very pleased. We'll be releasing this fall."

"Where you gonna sell, China?" The man from Angel Heart vineyards asks, eliciting a chuckle from the group.

I glance at Alison, who is shimmering fury. I can feel it sparking off of her, and it's directed at me. Before I can step in to put the asshole in his place, she clears her throat and speaks in a voice that demands attention. "While China is a burgeoning wine market that *I'll* definitely be exploring. This wine is special, and extremely limited. *I'll* be selling them by subscription for around $300 a bottle."

"You'll never get that," the Angel Heart guy says. "No one knows who you are. You have no reputation."

Alison smiles sweetly at him, but there's fire in her eyes. "The wine speaks for itself. And I bet you didn't have a reputation either, when you came to Angel Heart?"

"I had a pedigree." The guy looks to the others, who nod their approval. "I worked with some of the best wine-makers in California before coming to Napa. And while Case here may get his friends to buy wine that's not yours, good luck getting anyone to take a chance on an unknown selling premium wine."

"Yeah, this is the big leagues, honey. You're not in Kansas anymore," the leering asshole says, still eyeing her boobs. I want to throat-punch him.

Alison glares at the guy. "Never underestimate the power of a young woman from Kansas to flatten assholes," she says, clearly referencing the Wizard of Oz. I want to kiss her for that. "And for the record, I'm from Missouri, not Kansas, where we eat assholes for breakfast. With chopsticks."

The look on his face is priceless, and I want to fist-bump Alison, or at least give her a high-five for putting these dickwads in their place. But she's not through yet.

She gives all of us, including me, a dark smile, and extends her hand. "If you'll excuse me gentlemen, I have to go prepare my offering. Thank you for your time, it's been a pleasure."

The men are too surprised to not shake her hand, and when she gets to me, she grips my hand, fingers like talons. It might be intimidating if her hand wasn't so tiny, but I get the message, loud and clear. She's pissed as hell at me, and I'm sure to hear about it later. I open my mouth to speak but she cuts me off with a small shake of her head, and a look that would freeze a lesser man's balls.

When she's gone, Angel Heart guy, who I can see from his name tag is named Joey lets out a low whistle. "She's a firecracker."

The others chuckle and nod their agreement. "Yeah, I'd like to tap that," adds the fucker who's been eyeing her tits all night. "I bet she's an animal in bed."

"Fat girls always are," says the third.

For a minute, my vision spots, I'm so pissed. "I thought this was a winemaker's meeting," I grit, barely keeping my anger in check. "Not speed dating for asshats."

Joey's eyes widen before he scowls. "Calm down, Case, we're just having a little fun."

I step closer, flexing my hand to keep from forming a fist and breaking his nose. "At my brother's winemaker's expense." My voice drops low. "Let's get this clear, Joey. If I hear even a peep about Alison Walker that is in any way disparaging or anything less than sunshine and roses, you will feel the full force of the Case family name rain down upon you."

Behind me, titsperve scoffs. "And how far are you going to get now that Daddy's cut you off, and you're flat broke? Save your heroics for people who give a shit, Case."

One of them claps me on the back, and with a laugh, they all move off. *Karma* taunts the dark voice. I don't feel like mingling anymore, so I search for Alison, and find her in the corner behind the bar where a table has been set up for the winemakers to pour their tastes. "Can I help?"

Alison turns to face me. "You've helped *more* than enough, Nico," she says, voice shaking. "Please. Just leave me alone."

"But those guys were being assholes."

"And you weren't?" She steps closer and lowers her voice. I'm close enough to see that her eyes are glimmering with unshed tears. "You stomped all over me back there."

"No I didn't, I was helping you."

She makes a derisive noise in her throat. "That was not help. I asked you before, now I'm telling you. Leave. Me. Alone."

"But-"

She holds up a hand. "Go home Nico."

"But I'm your ride."

"I'll Uber."

"Like hell you will," I growl. "Not with the dark windy road and suspect drivers. No fucking way." I cross my arms. I'll leave her alone, but I'm not giving on this point. Not where her safety is concerned.

"I can handle myself. Now, leave me the *fuck* alone."

The bartender, who's as big as I am, steps out from behind the counter. "Is there a problem?"

Alison shakes her head. "No. He was just leaving."

Fuck. This guy is covered in tatts, and probably outweighs me by fifty pounds. I'm a big guy, but not that big, and I don't want to cause a scene. My presence here tonight has already caused a stir. I eye the bartender. I know when I've lost a battle. "Just make sure she gets a safe ride home."

Chapter Fifteen

Nico

*I*t's another hour before the winemaker's meeting breaks up. I've moved my bike into the shadows, because I don't want to look like I'm waiting for a parking lot fight. Although I'd gladly take on a half-dozen of these assholes, at least. No, my motives are much more altruistic tonight. I don't trust Uber drivers, not with all the crazy reports of women being kidnapped and raped, or worse, murdered. I just want to make sure Alison gets home in one piece. Safe.

She's one of the last to leave, and I'm heartened to see the bartender was good with his word. He's watching from the entrance. Alison scans the parking lot, and then, as if psychically aware, she turns and looks straight at me. I can't look away. Now that she's alone, I see the toll the evening has taken on her. She looks… defeated. My chest sinks, because how much of that is because of me?

She marches over, back ramrod straight. "I thought I told you to go home."

"And I thought I told you I don't trust Uber drivers."

She snorts. "What were you planning on doing, following me all the way home?"

"Yep."

She stares at me for a long moment without saying anything. Finally, she asks in a small voice, "Why?"

The answers flood my head. *Because against my better judgment, I like you. Because I don't want anything to happen to your pretty little ass. Because I couldn't live with myself if anything happened to you. Because I fucked up.* But I go with the safe answer, because all the answers bouncing around my head are far, far too dangerous to speak aloud. "Because Declan would kill me if anything happened to you."

Her shoulders slump the tiniest fraction, and I realize I've said the wrong thing, at least in her mind. My chest sinks further. I need to fix this. I *want* to fix this. I hate seeing her upset like this, with the fire snuffed out of her. *Start by apologizing, asshole*, the dark voice in my conscience tells me. That gives me pause. Now that I think about it, I can't remember ever apologizing to anyone but her. Maybe to my folks when I was a little kid, but never as an adult. *Never Apologize* could be the Case family motto. We're pretty much right, all the time. We're justified.

Ha. You're a fucking dumbass, my conscience counters. I clear my throat, pulse kicking erratically. I swallow, stomach clenching. "Look, back there… I was out of line. I'm sorry."

She eyes me with suspicion.

"I was trying to help. Those guys are douchebags, and one of them only looked at your tits-"

"You saw that too?" she says with a small laugh.

"I wanted to rip his balls off," I say darkly.

"I can handle myself, Nico." Her face pulls tight. "And you need to let me." She lets out a heavy sigh. "Look, I-"

"Let me make it up to you," I blurt. "Please?" I'm not used to pleading, not like this at least. The last time I begged for anything was when I was eleven, and my older brother Jason had tied the three of us up in the barn and was threatening bodily harm. I swore after that it would be the last time I begged for anything. I didn't beg Veronica to stay, hell, I didn't want her to. But this is different, and my instincts shout that the stakes are higher. "Please, Alison? I know this spot. We can grab some snacks and finish off the wine and just... talk." I open my hands, "No funny business." I cross my heart. "I swear." Unless she wants, and then I will funny business to her heart's content.

The Uber cab pulls up.

My heart thunks heavily against my ribs. Her eyes volley back and forth between me and the driver, then bounce to the bartender. The bartender pushes off the doorjamb he's leaning against and stalks to us. "Miss... are you okay? If he's bothering you, I can call the cops."

His comment must make up her mind, because she curses under her breath and waves him off. "It's okay. He can take me home. I appreciate your help."

"Are you sure?"

She meets my eyes. "Yes, thank you."

A weight lifts off my chest, relief coursing through my veins. "You won't regret it."

"Oh, I'm sure I already do," she says wryly, coming around the bike to accept the helmet I hold out for her.

Her face wrinkles as she messes with the chin strap and it's so. Damned. *Cute.* She climbs on behind me, refusing my hand, and the sense of home, the sense of rightness I feel as she presses against me is overwhelming. The bike rumbles to life beneath us. Nothing, *nothing* in my life has felt this right before, and I like the feeling of confidence that comes over me, like right now, in this moment, I'm invincible.

I pull to a stop at the *Napa Picnic Basket*, a mom and pop deli that tourists love. Even at seven-thirty, it's fairly crowded with people like me coming in to grab last minute snacks and picnic items before the sun sets. I make my choices- a selection of fruits, nuts, crackers, cheeses and meats I think will complement the wine from the cellar. I also grab a picnic cloth, a couple of acrylic tumblers, and a small knife and cutting board. Alison's eyes widen when she spies the bag. "Where are you going to put that?"

I flash her a grin and flick my eyebrows. "Bungee cords." I pull two out from a small saddle bag, along with a small canvas tarp with grommets punched in around the edges. In seconds, I've got our loot strapped down on the back of the seat. "Of course, you'll have to sit a little closer," I tease.

She grunts, but I see the hint of a smile twitching at the corner of her mouth. We settle in again, and I fire up the bike. I head north, planning to cut over to the 101 and a beach spot on the coast I like, but then I remember her pink fuck-me booties. Instead, I take the turnoff that takes us up Mt. Veeder, and to the property she's named Fieldstone Winery. Instead of parking my bike in the yard, I roll it right up to the edge of the vines- where I spotted a couple of large, low benches made from old redwood trees, worn smooth as marble from years of use and weathering. "I thought you were taking me someplace," she says, confusion in her voice.

"Change of plans." I unclip the sack and take it and the wine carrier to the bench. She's still standing by my bike, a funny expression on her face, when I've finished laying out the spread. "Is something the matter?"

"Why are you doing this?"

"Because, Alison Walker, I want to get to know you." I can tell from the tilt of her head she doesn't believe me. "For real."

She hesitates, then seems to give herself a shake, and she approaches, picking her way between the rocks and tufts of grass to join me on the bench. "This is... nice," she says, examining the spread between us.

"I wasn't sure what you liked, so I got a little bit of everything."

She waves an arm. "Oh I'm not very hungry."

"But you haven't eaten."

Her expression is cagey when she speaks again. "There was food for the winemakers in back," she says, not meeting my eyes.

She's lying. I know it. I've been around enough starving women to recognize the signs. "Alison," I say sternly, slicing open a pear, and topping a cracker with it and a slice of bleu cheese. I hold it out to her. "Don't bullshit me."

Chapter Sixteen

Alison

I don't know what to say. No one's ever called me out on my eating habits. Certainly, no one's ever been concerned. I give him a wan smile and take the cracker. A warm buzz of electricity runs up my arm and straight to my nipples when our fingers touch. They're sensitized from the ride. All of me is. It was all I could do to not grind my pussy into the seat as it vibrated beneath me. I'm achy, and I want to be touched. Strike that, I want to be fucked. Hard. I want to fuck away the shame, the humiliation, the anger at everything that transpired tonight. But I don't get to, because I made a promise to my sister.

I settle for food. It's dangerous for me, to eat my emotions, but at the moment it's my only option. "Okay, just one bite. But only one."

He scoffs and starts making another just like it.

It's good, the tang of the bleu cheese against the sweetness of the pear. It's sensuous, the way it melts in my mouth. Nico pours out the dregs of the white wine and offers me a glass. I take a sip and can't help but smile at the way the flavor plays with the pear and cheese. "This is so good." My mind goes to all the food the wine would enhance, pungent cheeses, salty salami, pate. He hands me another and I shamelessly grab it, because my God, I want that flavor again- exploding in my mouth, coating my tongue, setting off endorphins in my head.

"I love watching you eat," he says with a soft burr.

"Said no one ever," I scoff. There is absolutely nothing lovely about watching a fat girl eat.

"Alison," he says sharply. My eyes jerk to his. "Stop it. And for fuck's sake. Drop the 'I'm not hungry' act. You need food like anybody else."

Heat erupts in the pit of my belly and rockets through me. My cheeks flame, my chest is on fire, I feel like my head might explode from the shame of it. My issues with food are so fucked-up, and the fact that he's noticed, makes it ten times worse. Maybe a hundred. My hand shakes as I grab my wineglass and take a slow sip to steady myself. My appetite is gone now.

"Alison." This time, he says my name like a caress, and he takes my hand, thumb sliding hypnotically over the back of my hand. "Look at me."

I shut my eyes. He's asking too much, and if he sees the inside of me, if he discovers my secrets that hover so near the surface of my heart, what then? He could ruin me. But he's having none of my hiding. He tilts my chin up, forcing my gaze to his. His eyes are gentle, filled with concern, when I finally meet them. My heart squeezes painfully.

"Everyone deserves to enjoy food." Except me. I'm too cowardly to verbalize that, though. "And wine."

"Well, there's that," I admit, although I don't drink

very much. Empty calories are dangerous, and I promised myself I'd make healthy choices with my new body.

His mouth curves into a smile, and as soon as I return it, the energy between us shifts. Butterflies launch in my chest, thousands of them. His look becomes hungry, greedy even, and as he leans in, I know he's going to kiss me. I *want* him to kiss me. Kimmie's voice rings in my head, but I shut my eyes to it. His mouth is soft, sweet, even, gently probing. I lean in with a sigh, relishing the current of energy pulsing between us. His tongue teases my lower lip, flicking just inside, then away. Shamelessly, I chase after it, because who needs food when there's kissing this heavenly?

I'm flushed all over when we break apart, and a glance at Nico confirms he's just as aroused. But I can't help digging at him just a little. "I thought you said no funny business."

His eyes light. "Sorry, not sorry. There's just something about your mouth I can't resist."

"Except when I'm bossy mouth."

He chuckles and shakes his head, and when he looks at me again the heat in his eyes melts me, turns me right into a puddle. "That's when I want to fuck you silly."

"Oh."

Oh.

"Alison?"

My eyes flutter shut, in the hopes he'll kiss me again. "Mmmhmm."

"I really do want to talk."

"Talking is overrated," I mumble. Especially when we could be kissing.

His low rumble of a laugh pulls my eyes open. "Kissing after eating. And talking," he adds after I stare at him incredulously.

"Hmph," I grunt, and help myself to a slice of pear. "I'm eating, so you better start talking."

"So how did you get into wine?"

I stop mid-chew. Then gulp. If he asks about my childhood, I swear I'm getting up and leaving. "I majored in microbiology at Cornell. They had an enology program and it seemed fun. So I picked up a second major."

His eyebrows rocket up. "You got into wine because it seemed... fun?"

I lift a shoulder. "Sure, why not? Wine guys are nerdy, and they tend to be a fairly accepting crew." Except for Tommy.

"Except for the douchebags you met tonight," he says with a glower.

He's not wrong. "But the younger winemakers are different. More... diverse. Those guys? They'll be assholes until they die. And it sucks when they're jerks, but I know that I'm going to put this place on the map- not just because of the wine I know I can make, but because I'm going to do things differently."

"Hire an all-female crew," he fills in.

"Exactly." I pop a piece of salami in my mouth, and relish the salty fatty goodness coating my tongue, before taking a sip of the wine. I'm getting excited, I don't get to talk wine biz with many people, and he's the first out here, and I really do love this stuff. "Are you aware of the sexual assault rates in vineyards among laborers? And most of the time they go unreported because the women are afraid they'll lose their job. And to be honest, they work so damned hard, they should be the highest paid people in the vineyard. I'm trusting them with my grapes- my most precious commodity. Why wouldn't I compensate them handsomely?"

His brows knit together with a "Huh."

"Seriously, you're supposed to be a CEO and you haven't thought of this?"

"But how does it affect the bottom line?"

I roll my eyes. "There's more to running a company than the bottom line. Look where that's landed you all. You're not making art. *And* you're taking too much of a cut."

His head snaps back. "What do you mean?"

I can't help the snort that barrels out of my mouth. "Are you kidding? What do I mean? You're taking millions without lifting a finger, and the people who could royally fuck up your grapes, are barely making enough to feed themselves. Half are traveling more than two hours to come pick, because they can't afford to live here. And have you even *noticed* that vineyard labor is getting increasingly hard to come by because all your workers from Mexico are either getting harassed, or they can't obtain visas? How's *that* going to affect your bottom line when your grapes rot on the vine because there's no one to pick them?"

He repeats the brow knitting and 'huh'-ing with a shake of his head.

"You seriously haven't considered that? Even once?"

He narrows his eyes. "So how are you going to make a profit?"

"A collective."

"That's shit," he says with a dismissive wave of his hand. "That'll never work in Napa."

"Why the hell not?"

"Too expensive."

"It doesn't have to be."

"Collectives only work in developing countries where overhead is lower."

"They work because owners are investing in their employees," I say, voice rising. "What would happen if you paid your laborers a living wage? Better yet, since you have bazillions in profits, why not take a fraction of those profits, and offer to make down payments on homes, or condos, for your employees after a couple years of service? You'd have the best, most loyal vineyard labor in Napa, not to mention a public relations coup."

Nico stares at me, then shakes his head. "Sorry, sugar, business doesn't work that way. We both know that."

I don't want to let it go, and I'm pissed he's not on my side about this. But what should I have expected from a Case? I stand. "Well, it's a good thing I'm in charge here, because I plan to do just that. Then we'll see about business working that way. Now if you'll excuse me, I have some assholes to go crush." I start to pick my way back to the gravel, going as fast as my legs will carry me without rolling an ankle. Kimmie's right, leopards don't change their spots.

Chapter Seventeen

Nico

*J*eezus, how do things always manage to go south so quickly? *Fuck-up,* my conscience taunts. *Karma's a bitch.* "Wait," I call after her, rising to chase her down. "Ali, wait. Let's talk about something else," she slows, for a second, but then I realize it's because she wobbled on some loose gravel. Fuck. Fuckfuckfuck. "I can tell you why I've always been an asshole."

That stops her in her tracks, but she doesn't turn around. "Why? So you can give yourself some kind of absolution?" Her voice is as sharp as glass, and she shakes her head. "I'm not interested in being your confessor." She starts to move away again.

Something inside me screams at me that I have to convince her to stay, to give me a chance, that if I don't, I'm missing some kind of huge opportunity I'll regret for the rest of my life. And that it's going to take complete and total honesty from me. The realization scares the holy fuck out of me. I am the keeper of nasty dark secrets that should never see the light of day, but bringing them into the light is the only way to gain her trust, and so even though the back of my neck prickles with fear of what she'll say when she learns the depth of my treachery, I call after her. "No. So you can see the real me. The one that nobody knows."

She pauses, and I catch up to her, pausing within arm's reach. "How do I know you're not bullshitting me?"

"You don't. But the second you think I'm shitting you, you can ask me to leave, and I'll go." It's a risk, but I'm banking on her curiosity. I take another step forward, so close I could drop a kiss on her glossy dark hair. "Please? Come back and sit with me?"

A shiver races across her shoulders, and she lets out a deep sigh. "One chance, Case. You have one chance. The second I smell shit, you're out of here."

For the second time tonight, relief washes over me, followed by a hit of nauseating fear.

She spins and marches back to the bench, keeping her eyes focused on the horizon. Her ankles only wobble twice. When she reaches the bench, she uncorks the red wine and pours us full glasses.

"Didn't you serve this to them?"

She slides me a deadly glare. "They weren't worthy."

I toast her when she hands me the glass. "To crushing assholes."

She toasts back with a tight smile, and I wonder briefly, if I've just signed my own death sentence. There's no avoiding the truth that I'm an asshole too. But maybe she'll see it differently after I've spilled my guts. I taste the red, which she hasn't shared with me before. It's rich, complex, the kind of wine you contemplate. "Holy smokes that's good."

"I thought I'd call it Dark and Twisty."

"How about the Broodmeister?"

Alison's shoulder's shake. "That's a shit name. I've also thought about calling it Heathcliff."

"Heathcliff."

"The asshole from Wuthering Heights."

I recognize the title, but can't remember a damn thing about the book. "I'm pretty sure I skipped class that day."

"You skipped all the time," she says. "Didn't you?" she adds after a moment.

"Guilty as charged. Are you going to sit?"

She drops onto the bench. I'm torn, I want to sit next to her, but the picnic seems like a safe buffer. And I'm famished.

She slices a few pieces of the aged Reggiano I picked up, and pops a chunk into her mouth. We eat in silence, until she erupts in frustration. "Spill the beans, or I'm outta here. I have work left tonight."

"Oh?"

"Nope. You're not deflecting. Spill," she says, crossing her arms and narrowing her gaze. "Unless you were bull-shitting me."

"No, no," I respond hastily. I take a deep breath, then rise, unbuckling my jeans.

"What the fuck, Nico?" She jumps up, voice rising. "Is this some kind of a sick joke?"

"Nope," I stare at her grimly. "This is where the story starts."

"*With your dick?*" she squeaks.

"With this," I pull down the elastic of my black boxer briefs to just below my left hipbone. "Did you notice this during last night's fuckfest?" There's still enough light remaining I don't need a flashlight.

Her eyes drop to the two perfectly circular scars in the

crease between my leg and torso. "I thought they were some weird kind of ritual frat boy hazing thing," she murmurs, reaching out to touch them.

"Negative." If only. "Those were a gift from my older brother, Jason. And the twins have matching gifts under their left armpits." My heart is racing with the memory of that summer afternoon, and I have to fight the wave of nausea that settles in the pit of my stomach.

Alison's eyes are enormous, and her mouth forms an Oh. "Your brother did this to you?"

The horror in her voice drives straight to the darkest part of my soul. "Half-brother," I correct. "He's six years older than the three of us."

"When did this happen?"

"The summer we were eleven. There'd been other incidents before, but that summer, everything came to a head." I can still see my brothers tied up in the middle of the barn, Declan trying valiantly to be bold, Austin sniffling, trying to hold back tears he knew would only make Jason do worse things.

"What happened?" Her voice is terrible, filled with a kind of rage that I'd only expect from a parent.

I pull up the waistband and rebuckle my pants, and sit, forcing the vivid memory from my mind. "I won't go into the gory details-"

Alison follows suit. "But he should have been arrested, or-or something."

I appreciate her indignation on my behalf. "I think in this day and age, he would be, but he was bigger than us, and we were scared to tell."

"Said every victim ever," she says with such bitterness and anger I wonder what trauma she's experienced.

"He did get caught, later that summer, beating up the

son of one of the farmhands, and my parents sent him to reform school."

"Did it work?"

I shrug. "To be honest, I don't know. I steered clear of him whenever he was home, and plotted my revenge."

Understanding crosses her face. "So the fiancé…"

I nod. "I didn't mean to knock her up, I only wanted to screw over my brother in the worst possible way. The irony? I think she was plotting to screw us over the whole time, and I became her unwitting accomplice."

Alison snorts. "There's karma for you." She toes a rock with her pretty pink booties, and when she looks at me, it's with such intensity my heart clutches. "So tell me, Nicholas, what other asshole moves did you make as a result of your childhood trauma?"

I falter, because the expression on her face reaches into my soul, like she's seeing every single shitty thing I've ever done, and summing me up. "I-I'm not proud of my behavior. Not anymore," I amend. "I was an asshole. Hell, I still am, but hopefully less of one. I was a dick to pretty much everyone who walked. I didn't discriminate."

Her jaw clenches as she watches me, and for a moment, I think my confession won't be enough. "Ask me anything. I'm an open book."

For a long time, she just stares, eyes boring into me. "Tell me about high school," she finally asks.

"What I remember of it?" I wash down a cracker with some more wine. "I'm sure I was a dick, because I never missed an opportunity to mouth off. I remember parties, tons of parties. I was in the same class as Ronnie's younger sister Lara, and we all hung out at the country club our parents belonged to. To be honest, I spent as much time as I could getting stoned, so I don't remember a ton."

She makes a noise deep in her throat, then nods her head.

I hand her another cracker and she pops the whole thing in her mouth, finishing with wine, just like I did. The longer I study her, the more I can see the tension pulling around her mouth, and the way her shoulders hunch up toward her ears. "You okay?"

She pulls in a deep breath, then blows it out through puffed cheeks. "I was bullied in high school," she finally admits in a quiet voice. "By a group of rich, entitled, mean kids."

"Assholes like me," I supply.

She lets out a bitter laugh and shakes her head. "Yeah. I guess you could say that."

"Point them out to me someday and I'll pound their faces."

Her eyes cut to mine, and I don't like what I see there—the hurt, the anger, the *hate*. What did they do to her that she still harbors that much pain? Although I'm one to talk, given my feelings about my older brother. I'd just as soon punch his face in than talk to him. "Do you think people can change?" Her eyes search mine, and I suddenly have the feeling of walking a tightrope. That if my answer isn't up to snuff, she'll show me the door, and I'll never get to have those fuck-me pink booties wrapped around my neck.

I search for the words. "If I say that I think people can change, then I have to leave room for the possibility that my brother might have changed."

"And you don't want to believe that," she finishes.

"I don't," I admit. "There's a satisfaction in holding onto my anger."

"But then by logical conclusion, it means you're still an asshole, and that you'll always *be* an asshole, no matter what."

I don't like that. "But I'm better than he is."

She snorts. "Now I smell the bullshit. Either people change, or they can't. You can't have it both ways."

She has a point, but the implications make me very uncomfortable. "Okay then, I think people can change, but I think most won't."

"And which are you?"

My heart makes its way down to my toes then crams itself up in my throat. There's an ache in my chest I can't name. "I…" I let out a puff of air, then swallow. The lump in my throat remains. "I want to change. I-I want to be better." I want to be worthy of her approval. I want Alison to look at me with the world in her eyes. I take another deep breath, and move from my spot on the bench, and come to kneel before her. I take her hands in mine. She's guarded, still, but she hasn't pushed me away either. "Alison… Ali… you make me want to be a better man. The best kind of man."

She sucks in air, lips parting in surprise. "Now you're shitting me for reals."

I rise up and frame her face with my hands, taking her mouth. She opens to my tongue with the sweetest sigh, and I take my precious time exploring her, devouring her. Her foot kicks out and wraps around my waist, and with a guttural noise I deepen the kiss, my hands slipping under her jacket to caress the curve of her breasts. I tease her nipples through the thin fabric, relishing the weight of her resting in my palms. "I will be most happy to show you all the ways I'm most definitely not shitting you," I murmur, pinching her nipples in the way I know drives her wild.

"Show me," she answers. "Right now."

Chapter Eighteen

Alison

I drop my head back with a groan, relishing the sting on my nips all the way to my clit. I'm so wet, I'm sure there's a damp spot on my leggings, but ask me if I care? I don't, not with Nico's tongue sliding against mine, teasing in and out until I can barely stand it.

I can't believe I'm doing this. Seriously, I think I've lost my marbles. Kimmie would tell me I'm suffering from a bad case of Stockholm syndrome and pour ice water over my head. Maybe even slap me. And she'd be right to, because who fucks their former tormentor? Am I stupid to believe him when he tells me I make him want to be better? When he promises to show me he's absolutely not shitting me?

Honestly, the man makes it hard to harbor a grudge, and not just because his ass is so fine and his abs are perfectly cut, and he kisses in a way that makes my pussy instantly wet. I get the feeling he's really trying. Why would he tell me that shit about his brother if he was just playing me? And if he's struggling to forgive his brother, shouldn't I try to forgive him too? It's easy when he kisses me like I'm his last breath, his only lifeline.

What would Kimmie say?

Kimmie would say run, and I'm doing just that. But not in the direction she'd want. Nope, for once in my life, I'm taking what I want, because I deserve to be happy, even if it's only for a moment. And dammit, I'm so sick of living in the darkness, of apologizing for who I am and who I've been. And maybe this... *thing*... between us is an opportunity for a fresh start- for both of us. Because, my God, his touch drives me wild, makes me wet with need, obliterates my self-doubt. Who wouldn't want that kind of goodness in their lives?

"Nico," I murmur between kisses.

"Mmm," he growls, nipping at my collarbone.

"We should take this inside."

"Hell no. I'm taking you right here."

"Outside?" I squeak, pulling away. "Are you crazy?" It's getting dark, but I can still see the hunger written all over his face.

"Only for you, angel. And I want you to think of mind-blowing orgasms every time you walk by this bench.

"But-but," I sputter, unable to come up with a compelling reason why we shouldn't. "Someone might see us," I finish lamely.

"No one is up here but us."

"A-and raccoons and coyotes."

His laugh skates across my skin, leaving delicious goosebumps. "They give no shits about us. But if you want me to stop..." His voice trails off as he pulls away, an amused smile pulling his mouth wide. He pulls my leg from his waist, and slowly removes my ankle boot. "Promise me someday, you'll wear these with a skirt? So I can bury my face in your pussy while you wrap your legs around me in nothing but these?"

I'm pretty sure, my heat levels just reached supernova levels. I don't even own a skirt, but I'll order one first thing tomorrow just so we can do that.

He removes my other boot. "Have you ever gone skinny dipping?"

I snort. "No. I've never been naked outside."

"We'll have to do that, too." I'm not sure where he's going with all this future planning shit, but part of me thrills at the idea of planning things with him. "Pants off," he orders in a tone of voice that brooks no argument, and I'm only too happy to oblige, especially when I see his hand come to rest on his belt buckle.

I reach out, hand covering his. "Let me do that."

He opens his hands and lets me have free reign. I fiddle with the buckle, then the top button, then the rest of the buttons, because damn if he's not wearing vintage 501's. I'm impatient and greedy to see his cock, to wrap my fingers around its girth and feel the slick heat of him in my palm. He helps me push down his jeans and boxer briefs, and I gasp like a kid opening a birthday present when his cock springs free, jutting between us thick and long. I run a fingertip along the sensitive underside, stroking up to the flared edge of his crown. This is better than any vibrator. His cock jerks at my touch and he hisses out a breath. I glance up. His face is taut, eyes feverish and focused on my hand, it's sexy as fuck, and I'm so wet, my thighs are slick with it.

I stroke back down and take his balls in my palm, using my fingernails to scratch the sensitive spot at the back. He makes an animal sound that ricochets through me like wildfire. I have to squeeze my thighs together because I need friction from somewhere, and touching him is making me so aroused, it's going to take nothing for me to come. "Lie back on the bench," he growls. "Drop your legs to either side."

My heart pounds at his order. He'll be able to see the bruises he left the night before. He'll also see that I shaved my pussy this morning. I've only done it once before, when I was in a self-experimental phase- the maintenance is kind of a pain, but I kept fantasizing about his cock sliding through me with no friction.

"You shaved," he says, voice dry as grass in September.

I grin and shrug. "Looks like it."

"I like how dirty your mind is, Alison."

I love how he says my name. It's sexy and sensual and it hints of orgasms. "I prefer to call my mind beautifully imaginative." It should be from the thousands of dollars I've spent reading romance novels since I found them one Saturday in the library when I was thirteen.

His laugh fills the air. "I love it," he says. "And I suppose your beautiful imagination wants me to eat you up?"

"Oh yes, please," I breathe, spreading my legs wider. A light breeze dances through, and my skin erupts in goose-bumps. My already sensitized clit, throbs, a bundle of nerves eager for the soft heat of his tongue.

He bends, staring up at me, and I can't help but watch as he lowers his face to my cunt. I cry out as he slowly licks up my slick seam, tongue coming to rest on my clit. I can't look away, I'm mesmerized by the look on his face. It's reverent, hungry, and aroused, all at once. I commit this moment to memory, tucking it away for future examination, and cry out again when he repeats his movements. His eyes never leave my face. My hips rock into him, and he licks harder, somehow understanding my need for more friction, for a harder touch. His hands come to the outside of my thighs, squeezing hard, pulling me closer, the ache builds and builds, and I only break eye-contact when my orgasm explodes like a starburst, and my vision spots. I let go with a shout, maybe the loudest sound I've ever made, because we're outside and who's gonna hear us, and God, it just feels so damn liberating to yell. I'm shaking all over, and this time, my shout dissolves into a fit of delighted giggles.

He's grinning when he raises his head and pulls me forward, lining my opening up with his cock. "You okay?" He asks, his cock nudging at my entrance. I want him inside me, filling me up. I want that feeling of feeling so full, I think I can't take it. I want the ache that only a cock can give.

I grin back. "Never better."

He thrusts into me hard. Hard enough, my butt slides along the smooth bench, and thank god it's smooth, because I checked before I set my bottom on it. The last thing I want is an ass full of splinters.

He pulls me back, thrusting again, and I swear he touches the core of me. I wrap my legs around his waist, and hang on for dear life as his thrusts become more force-ful. I brace up on an elbow and pull him down for a kiss, but not before I catch a glimpse of his cock slick with my arousal sliding through my bare pussy. It's erotic as fuck, and it feels so damn good, I'm tempted to put in the effort to maintain this level of smoothness. I taste myself on his tongue, and I swear it makes me even wetter. I feel like a goddess who's been worshipped fully, and I'm overcome with the desire to be fully naked in the moonlight, like some sort of pagan ritual. "Wait," I say, as I wriggle out of my jacket and lie back on the bench to shimmy out of my top.

His low chuckle only encourages me, and I hear the soft whisper of his clothes sliding against his skin, and then flying to the ground to join mine. I pop the front clasp on my bra and free my breasts. "Much better," he acknowledges, bringing first his hands, then his mouth to my nipples. He slides his hands under my ass, and pulls me up onto his thighs, and resumes his thrusts.

I gasp at the intensity that the newer angle provides. "Holy shit, Nico," I say tightly, clutching his forearms.

"You're so good, Alison, so tight, so wet."

My orgasm starts to build from someplace deep inside me, springing to life with each punishing thrust, each slide out against my clit. "It's too much, I can't take it," I say, even though I'd kill him if he stopped now. But I am just the tiniest bit afraid I'm never going to be the same again after this.

"You can, Alison. I promise. It's gonna be so good."

And I believe him. I can hear the reverence in his voice, the promise. And most importantly, the intensity that tells me he's as close as I am, and that when we explode, we might just trigger a goddamned earthquake. I cry out with each thrust, a tingling, pressure-filled sensation that builds and builds, and erupts when he brushes his thumb against my clit. I convulse around him, pussy rippling in waves that consume my whole body. And he's right there with me. He thrusts so hard, so deep, I feel the vibrations in my sternum. His shouts mingle with mine, piercing the darkness, yet being swallowed by the vastness of the acreage. And I wonder, as I float back to earth, if the old adage about a tree falling in the woods, holds the same for shouting orgasms.

Chapter Nineteen

Nico

I'm not exactly sure how, but somehow, we manage to make our way back to the trailer with all our clothes and the picnic. It's hours before we actually make it back to the bedroom though. Because first, I take her on the couch, then on the kitchen counter, and on the tile wall in the shower, with her foot braced against the built in bench. The old-fashioned clock glows half-past-two when we collapse onto the bed, wrapped in our towels.

"Work crew arrives at six tomorrow," she murmurs, snuggling into the crook of my arm.

"No chance we could blow them off?" It's more of the same, and they're experienced. They can get started without Alison. "We're probably two days away from thinning the rest of the vines."

"Nope." She drapes an arm across my midsection.

I think that means she's not kicking me out to the couch tonight. At least I hope so. I like the feel of her warm body snuggled against mine. Ronnie wasn't a cuddler. She said it gave her face wrinkles. "So, maybe I should hit the couch," I suggest.

Her eyes stay shut, but her mouth lifts at the corners. "You can, if you like. It's up to you."

The old Rush song with the Oscar Wilde quote pops into my mind. *I can resist anything but temptation.* I should go. I've bared too much of my soul tonight. And while I can't deny the lightness of spirit that comes with allowing deep, dark secrets to come to light, it doesn't wipe out years of being a first-rate dick, and if Alison looks too closely, she may discover she doesn't like what she sees, after all. Chemistry be damned. I push up to an elbow, with every intention of rolling off the bed and marching myself down the hall, but she's started to snore lightly, already fast asleep. And it's so. Damned. Cute. And her body is so soft and warm next to mine, I can't bring myself to get up just yet. I drop back to the mattress and run a hand across the swell of her hip. So soft, so inviting. So tempting. I'll just shut my eyes for a few minutes before I go back to the couch...

―――――

"No offense, but Dark and Twisty is a terrible name for a premium wine."

Ali scowls and makes a cute little growly noise of frustration, and turns back to her laptop. "No one asked you, pretty boy."

I step behind her and sweep her hair off her neck, planting a slow kiss at the base. "Just sharing my CEO expertise... bossy mouth."

She growls again. "When I want your expertise, I'll ask for it."

I kiss her neck again, and peer over her shoulder. "What are you looking at?"

"Barrels."

"Why not use the barrels in the cellar?"

"You mean the ones with wine in them?" she asks with a bite of sarcasm.

"You'll be bottling that soon."

She swivels to stare at me through narrowed eyes. "Are you trying to CEO me again?"

I smirk and bend, caging her in, and taking her mouth for a brief kiss. "I may be trying to seduce you."

She gives me a playful shove and swivels back. "Because going all Alpha is the key to winning any woman's heart."

"It is yours," I blurt before my brain catches up with my mouth.

She freezes. We both do. We've been living in this fantasy realm for the better part of a month now, sneaking fucks in the vineyard or the crushing pad between equipment delivery, or when the workers on Declan's farmhouse have left. For the most part, we've been alone up here on the mountain. The vineyard isn't open for business, and there's no tasting room, so we don't have tourists or buyers stopping by for a taste. It's been the two of us hidden away on the mountaintop, and it's been fucking amazing. But we both know it can't last- Declan will be showing up at some point, and the Chardonnay harvest is mere weeks away. This is merely the calm before the storm.

"I…" Alison's head drops and she huffs out a breath, slowly swiveling the chair back around to face me. "There's something you should know about me."

My heart yo-yos. Her face is so serious, pained, even. "Yes?" I ask, throat suddenly dry.

"I'm divorced."

I let out a relieved laugh. "Is that all? I thought you were going to tell me you had cancer or something."

Her mouth curves up, but it's not a smile. "What I'm trying to say is…" she sucks in a breath. "I don't really have a heart to give. Not anymore."

It takes a full minute for me to realize the meaning in her words. And to be honest, I'm not sure how I feel about her declaration. Relieved, yes. Disappointed, yes. Wanting to throat punch her ex, who obviously is an asshole, definitely yes. I wave a hand. "Oh, that. Hyperbole, angel."

Her face visibly relaxes, and she tilts her head, her eyes crinkling as she smiles. "Okay, just checking. 'Cause this-" She waves between us. "Is nice. Really nice. But I can't see us going anywhere. Can you?"

"No, no not at all," I agree with a shake of my head. Then why do I feel like I've just been sucker punched?

Chapter Twenty

Alison

*I*t would be so easy to fall for him. Kimmie was right, it's a slippery slope, and I can feel myself slipping a little more each day, in spite of my declaration. I was surprised by his reaction, and if I'm honest with myself, even the tiniest bit disappointed. Because things between us are... surprisingly easy. In spite of the secrets still piled up between us. All the more reason this can't ever go beyond a wild sexy late summer fling.

It's barely light out, as I stretch and roll over for a little morning hanky-panky. Only Nico's side is empty. "Nico?" I call, pushing up. Nico is *not* an early riser. Not remotely. So I immediately dismiss the idea that he's up making himself a cup of coffee, and me a cup of tea. He's not the 'surprise me with breakfast in bed' type, which is fine with me. I'm not that type either. I'm an early riser and breakfast is over-rated, as far as I'm concerned. "Nico?" I call again after listening for him. I don't hear him anywhere.

And then, I hear knocking- persistent knocking- at the door. My stomach drops as my imagination conjures up all manner of awful. Did something happen to Nico? Is he sick? Injured? Or dear God, is there a fire? Did something happen to the grapes?

The knocking continues as I throw back the covers and head to the bathroom for my robe. My pulse quickens as I secure the tie and hurry down the hall to the front door. I offer up a silent prayer to the universe that everyone I love is okay. I fling open the door and blink. Nico's standing on the other side of a car that's definitely not mine. And... I blink again forcing my synapses to fire.

The familiar face smiles. "Alison?"

"Yeah?" I answer stupidly, and then my brain wakes up. Fucking hell, it's Declan, looking a little worse for wear, but it's definitely him. "Holy shit," I mutter. Then I look down. Fuck. My robe barely covers my ass. "Hooooooooly, *holy* shit." I start running at the mouth... because it's too early to be thinking clearly. "What in the hell are you doing here?" I look from him to Nico and back again. "Did I do something wrong? I swear, if you don't like something, blame him." I point to Nico, completely okay with the fact that I'm shamelessly throwing him under the bus. I glare at him. "I never should have listened to you about rearranging the crushing pad."

Nico raises his hands looking from me to his brother, and damn if he's not smirking. "What? Don't look at me. She's the winemaker. She's calling the shots."

Fucker.

I immediately think of all the delicious ways I can spend the day torturing him.

Declan shakes his head, with an expression that sends dread shooting right into my bones. "I know it's early, but I have a full day. Can you show me around? I want to see where we are."

I gulp. "Right now?"

He gives me an exasperated look. "Some clothes would be nice."

Shit. This could not be more embarrassing. My first face to face meeting with my boss and I'm half-naked and sexed up from a night of lovemaking. "Yes, of course. I'll be right out." I let the screen slam behind me and tear down the hall. *Shit oh shit oh shit shitshitshit.* What if he doesn't like what I've done with the grapes? Or how I've supervised the construction on the farmhouse? What if he decides I'm a rank amateur and sacks me on the spot? I brace my hands on the counter in the bathroom and glare at myself. "Pull yourself together, girl. You are badassery embodied. He hired you because you know what you're doing, and you're damn good at it." I nod emphatically at my reflection.

I dress quickly, grabbing a clean pair of jeans instead of my beat up work overalls, a pair of sturdy boots, and for confidence- my motorcycle jacket over a *Ramones* tee shirt. It's too early for lipstick, but I fluff my bangs I gave myself last week, and pull the rest of my hair into a ponytail. I've got this. *I've Got This.*

When I join Declan in the yard, Nico's nowhere to be found. It's on the tip of my tongue to ask where Nico's disappeared to, but I stop myself just in time. Inquiring about Nico would be a dead giveaway. And I'll miss him in the vineyard this morning. I've been walking the lots several times a day, getting to know what's ripening first, making a plan for harvest, ordering equipment, cleaning and recleaning everything so it's ready when we start picking. I can feel the anticipation building daily. Harvest time is magic, it's why I chose to become a winemaker, and I'm simultaneously thrilled and terrified for our inaugural harvest. "Where do you want to start?" I ask, already formulating a plan of where I'll take Declan first.

He walks in a circle, hands on his hips, surveying the buildings and the trees in the distance. Wispy pink clouds color a robin's egg blue sky. "How about with the vines? I think a walk would do me some good."

Good man. Always start with the vines. They matter the most. I can't help the grin of approval that pulls my mouth up. "Excellent place to start." I cut through the barnyard to the Chardonnay vines first. "I think we're about four weeks out? As you know, it's not an exact science." I palm a cluster. "They're still pretty hard, and the seeds are still pretty green." I pull of a grape and bite it open, spitting out the pulp. It's cheek puckering tannic. I squish the remaining pulp and push up the seeds. "See how they're still hard? We want them brown and starting to go mushy."

I offer him what's in my hand, but he waves it away. "That's why I hired you. I don't know shit about this process."

I suspected as much, but to hear the heir to one of the biggest wine fortunes in the world blow off the *entire* process of turning grapes into wine, is more than a little irritating. It gives me new appreciation for Nico's interest in what's happening with the vines.

"So I could make cougar juice, and you wouldn't care, so long as I made a profit?" I say with more than a little disgust.

His eyes snap to mine. "That bother you?"

"Of course." I give him one of those 'are you a fucking idiot' looks. "I'm a winemaker. No. Strike that. I'm an artist. No." I shake my head. "Strike that too. I'm a fucking magician. And I will make you money, don't worry. But not by taking shortcuts and making a subpar product."

He stares at me, then bursts out laughing. "I knew you were a firecracker. Holy shit, no wonder you're driving Nico crazy." He laughs again. "You're perfect."

Something stabs in my heart. I'm driving Nico crazy? I thought… oh, fuck… I thought. I want to vomit. But how could we, how could he… I'm driving him crazy? A lump grows in my throat, one I can't swallow away. I've been such a fool. I blink rapidly, biting my cheek, and somehow manage to smile. I swallow again, unsure if my voice will work when I speak. "Let's hike down to the Cabernet lot, shall we?"

I force my attention to the grapes, bringing Declan up to speed on our pruning and thinning practices, and why. I share what we're noticing about ripening patterns on the steep slope and how I think we'll manage that during the harvest. The top lots will ripen first, so we'll pick, and slowly work down the steep hill to the bottom Cabernet vines, which I expect will be ready in late October, or maybe even early November.

"Shall we go taste the barrels?" I ask when we've reached the bottom elevation of the property. It will take a good 20 minutes to hike back.

"At seven-thirty in the morning?" Declan asks, incredulous.

I shrug. "Sure. Why not? You can spit if you prefer."

He snorts. "As if."

"I knew I liked you." I grin. Seriously, I could not have landed a better boss. Except for the small fact that I'm fucking his brother, and I'm pretty sure he'll terminate me on the spot if he finds out. And the other small issue that Declan doesn't know I've forced Nico to work for me this entire time.

He doesn't look twice at the crushing pad layout- something Nico and I have gone round and round about for days. Like, seriously? Why did I bother stressing about it? You can lead a horse to water...

We make our way to the wine cellar, and I thrum with expectation. Once the vineyard is officially open for business, I can't wait to bring VIP groups down here for special tastings. I've already set it up with a seating area complete with rugs and leather couches, small sitting areas for people to gather for education and fucking fantastic wine. It will be more intimate when there are more barrels down here, but I could easily host a small gathering of thirty or forty people, complete with candles and nibbles.

Declan lets out a low whistle when he takes it all in. "You've been holding out on me Alison. You've got serious vision."

"Of course I do," I snort. "We're gonna kill it up here."

"I love it."

I grab a couple of tasting glasses and a wine thief from a shelf and lead Declan to the first barrel of white. I fill our glasses and we swirl. His reaction makes me giddy. "See?" I'm bouncing on my toes. "I told you it was amazing."

He grins at me. "Think you can duplicate it?"

"Or better."

I fill him in on my plans for this year- to test the limits of the grapes- with steel and various kinds of oak barrels, for different kinds of fermentation. Once we've established what the grapes can do, then we can decide on a direction. "I have a whole spreadsheet on my laptop I can show you."

"No need." Declan waves me off. "Clearly you've got it under control.

I'm pleased, but also just the tiniest bit disappointed. I

assumed that as the vineyard owner, he'd take an active interest, not just delegate the whole kit and caboodle to me. I start to tell him that Nico has been a great sounding board for the process, and that I couldn't have come up with it without him, but I don't want to arouse his suspicion. And sadly? I think he wouldn't care. He's... distracted. That much, I can see. The vineyard is the last thing on his mind. "Everything okay?"

"What... with me? Yeah, of course. Everything's fine."

"You're as full of shit as your brother."

He smiles at that. "That's us. Just call us the shit brothers."

"So you'll be helping Nico turn the compost pile later today?"

His laughter echoes off the wall. "Sure." He extends his hand. "I like you, Alison. Danny said you're as smart as they come, and I know I'm paying you a fortune, but I still think I got the better end of the deal."

Chapter Twenty-One

Nico

*I*t's a little after nine when I return from my enforced breakfast with a bag of groceries for the fridge. Alison is working so hard now, during the lead-up to harvest, that I try and help where I can. I still cook for shit, and I probably got too many frozen meals, but she's never complained. I think, I *hope*, she's grateful to have one less thing on her plate.

She's sitting at her laptop futzing with the spreadsheet I helped her make for all the different barrels she wants to use with this year's harvest. I don't honestly know how much will actually get released, but she's got good instincts about testing the capacity of the grapes. It's not like there's a history of the vineyard she can study, and see what's worked in past years. We're- *she's* starting off fresh here.

I have to keep reminding myself that I'm not part of this project. I'm not even here permanently. In fact, I've probably overstayed my welcome. It's only a matter of time before Dec kicks me out and I have to go land somewhere else until I can figure out my next move.

I drop the groceries on the counter and then come to sweep the hair from her neck so I can kiss one of my favorite spots. "How'd it go?"

She lets out a groan of frustration, and swivels around. "He doesn't give a shit, Nico. It's… disappointing. I thought for sure he'd have some kind of input. I mean, he approves of the choices I've made, but it's like his brain is somewhere else. Like I could tell him I planned to rip out all the vines after harvest, and he'd just wave me on."

"He's a real-estate guy. He's used to delegating."

"But so are you, but you don't… you…" she shakes her head. "It doesn't matter." Her face is full of gratitude when she raises it to meet my eyes. "Thanks for your help."

I brace my hands on the arms of the chair, trapping her. I bring my mouth to her neck, trailing kisses along the sensitive cord and up to the hollow at her ear. "Is that your way of buttering me up after throwing me under the bus this morning?"

"Are the groceries your way?" she shoots back when she sees the sack on the counter.

"I love you Alison." It just slips out, because her wit, her fire, her sparkling sense of humor cracks me up. And nobody is more surprised than me. It wasn't like I woke up this morning and thought 'hey, I'll tell Ali I love her today.' I only woke up early because I had a weird dream and I heard a car pull up, and when I realized it was Dec, I just had to fuck with him.

She doesn't freeze this time, she just stares at me, eyes searching mine, penetrating into the deepest part of me. And then she laughs. A delighted, giddy sound, and she wraps her hand around my neck and pulls me into a kiss. It's sweet and gentle and sensuous, and very quickly things heat up between us, and she's reaching for the button on my jeans. I don't care that her sole response was to laugh, because her hand is stroking my cock, and all I want is to be inside her, showing her that I fucking adore her.

I pull her up and lead her down the hall. "Declan's car is gone, and we don't have deliveries until after lunch today."

"But what about the construction guys?" she asks breathlessly.

"You'll have to promise not to scream my name when you come."

She kicks off her boots and scoots into the middle of the bed, watching hungrily as I pull my tee shirt over my head and toss it to the floor, next to where I've dropped my jeans. She shimmies out of her jeans, kicking them aside as soon as her legs are free, and reaches for her shirt.

I crawl toward her. "Let me."

I start by stroking up her thigh and catching the hem pulling it up enough to tease at the soft skin beneath. "Someday we're gonna talk about your misguided affection for the Ramones," I say as I pull the shirt over her head, and nuzzle my way down her neck to the valley between her breasts. My fingers find the clasp of her bra and flick it apart. I could lose myself forever in the full, sweet softness of her tits, and I tease and lick until she sighs and her hips rock beneath me.

"And then we're gonna talk about your misguided affection for Wham and the soundtrack of Moana," she squeezes out between the sexy little moans she makes.

"Don't judge. And besides, you like jazz." I take a nipple into my mouth, teasing the tip with my tongue.

She snorts, then gasps as I gently bite. "There's nothing jazzy about Wham."

I trail kisses down her belly, and push her legs apart so

that I can get to her pussy, which is slick with heat. "But George Michael recorded a jazz album." I bend and take a long, slow lick up her seam, just how she likes, slowly circling her clit. "Yes," she pants. "That feels so good. And I like Miles Davis. Big difference." Her voice rises over the last two words as she comes apart on my tongue, and then she laughs again- a joyous, melodic sound that worms its way into my soul and takes up residence.

"That's all you have to say?" I tease after she's come down. "That Miles Davis is jazzier than George Michael? You're going to have to do better than that if you want my cock in you."

Her eyes narrow. "You wouldn't."

I roll onto my back so she can see just how hot I am for her, and stroke myself slowly. "You can't be dissing George and the boys if you want... this." I eye her, waiting for her next move. She doesn't disappoint.

She crawls over me, and brackets my thighs with her knees. "You sure you want to be making ultimatums like that?" she returns with a devilish smile, dipping her head to slide her tongue up my cock. "Two can play that game, and I happen to know how bad your cock-" She takes the crown of me into her mouth, rolling her tongue around the circumference, and applying just enough suction my eyes roll into my head. "Wants this," she murmurs, and does it a second time.

And she's right. I want her mouth on my cock in the worst way. She licks at me, all the while talking smack about Wham, and my poor taste in music, and when I think I can't take it anymore, I pull her up to straddle me, and thrust into her slick channel with everything I have. Only this time, I pull her against my chest, and using an old self-defense move, I roll us so that she's on her back and I'm on top, sinking into her. "You're not the only one with tricks up your sleeve, angel," I growl before taking her mouth in a claiming kiss. She meets me thrust for thrust, groaning into my mouth as I fuck her hard and fast, then slow, then thrusting and rocking so that when I pull out my cock slides against her clit, giving her the friction I know she craves.

And the best part? She's grinning from ear to ear when I break the kiss long enough to look down at her. Her pupils are blown, so that her eyes are practically black, and for a moment, I pause, because I just have to look at her, commit her complete and total enjoyment to memory. "I love you too, Nico," she whispers so quietly, I almost miss it. Something weird and achy throbs below my sternum, spreading across my chest. It's tight and hot, and it grows as we lie tangled together, and I begin to slide home. And as her breath becomes sharper, shorter, and mine joins hers, we climax together in a chorus of cries and laughs, and the thing in my chest releases and I'm filled with the most incredible sense of lightness, of rightness, of... peace.

Chapter Twenty-Two

Nico

*S*omething's up with Dec. I've never seen him like this, pushing himself to the brink the way he has since he's arrived, saying barely two words to me, and virtually ignoring Alison. She's sent us to turn compost, because she wants us out of her hair, and Declan needs something to do, because he's driving us both crazy.

Finally, I jab my fork into the pile. I'm not a touchy-feely guy, especially where my brothers are concerned, but this shit has to stop. "Wanna talk about it?"

Dec keeps tossing manure onto the pile and turning it as if I haven't spoken. "Nope," he finally grunts.

Jeezus, he has it bad. But if I've learned one thing up here, it's that hard work cleanses you, clears your head, helps you find perspective. "I've been there, you know."

He throws down the pitchfork and turns with a glare, hands fisted. For a hot second, I think he's gonna punch me, and instinctively I drop my fork too, ready to fend off a blow. But then the fight leaves him and he sags. I've never seen him look so defeated. "Yeah, I know." He picks up his fork, and attacks the pile again.

I resume turning the pile, and soon enough we settle into a rhythm of stab, pull, toss.

"Emmaline's mother just died of Alzheimer's," he says. And bit by bit, as we work together, the story comes out. There's no doubt about it, my brother the player is nursing a broken heart, and I have no idea how to help him. Because fuck, Veronica humiliated me, but I didn't love her. And now that I have something to compare it to with Alison, something that… means something to me, I can see even more clearly that I was more interested in sticking it to Jason than I was about loving Veronica. And I guess that makes me the worst kind of asshole. There must be a special place in the circles of hell for men that marry someone out of spite, for revenge.

Declan pauses from his storytelling. "This is off-topic, but have you been talking to Veronica lately?"

"Fuck, no," I scoff. "If I never speak to her again it will be too soon."

"So you have no idea why she might be calling?"

I jab my fork in the shrinking pile, stomach clenching. "She's calling *you?*" I shake my head. "She probably saw the article in Winemaker's monthly."

"That's what I thought, too. But I was surprised, because last I heard she was holed up in Senator Whelan's house in Malibu."

"Well it's no longer my fucking problem, I've moved on."

"Oh?" There's weight in Declan's voice, and curiosity. "You got a rebound thing going?"

I freeze, knuckles white on the handle. I'm not ready to take this thing with Alison public. Especially not with Dec.

But then again, there's going to be speculation because of the pictures in *Winemaker's Monthly*. And maybe that's not such a bad thing. But I still lie to my brother. "Nah." And then I change the subject.

We finish the pile and Declan heads back to his makeshift setup in the unfinished farmhouse. So far, he hasn't commented on the fact that I'm sharing space with Alison. As far as he's concerned, I'm still sleeping on the couch. Alison finds me in the barn, putting away the tools. "Walk the lots with me? I need to check the sugars."

I turn with a grin, because in addition to checking the sugars, it's code for sneaking in some naughty time at the far corner of the lot. She's wearing her work overalls and a new sports bra- one with cups. I trace a finger along the strap and down, skimming the tops of her breasts. "This new?"

She flicks up her brows and gives me a naughty smirk. "Easier access." She winks and turns, swinging her hips with more sass than usual. My cock thickens in anticipation, because hell, yes. She takes her damn time checking the Chardonnay, torturing me with sideways glances, brushing my ass, and generally teasing me to a state of frustrated arousal, dancing out of range whenever I reach for her. She finally lets me catch her when we reach a picnic table halfway through the Cabernet lots. "Some might call you a cock tease," I growl pulling her in for a kiss. She tastes of tannic grapes, but it's the sweet notes underneath that drive me wild, that make me never want to stop kissing her.

She unsnaps the straps of her overalls, and they fall to her hips. I follow suit, dropping my jeans. We have vineyard quickies down to a science, and while they're never the same, we can't risk getting caught. This time, she turns and bends over the table, and I step behind her, yanking her overalls past her hips, revealing a black lace thong. "Someone's been shopping online," I murmur, palming the soft flesh of her ass and slipping my hand between her thighs. As always, she's soaking and ready. I slip a finger, then two, inside her, pumping as she grinds into me. "I've been thinking about this all morning," she confesses.

"This too?" I ask as I slide my fingers against her clit. My cock is like steel, and impatient to get in on the action. "I love seeing you like this, all worked up, and with sexy underwear underneath your work clothes."

She looks back over her shoulder with a wide smile, and I think I fall a little harder for her. I push down my boxer briefs. "Spread your legs a little wider, angel."

She does so with a shimmy. And I step up, sliding her thong to the side and nudging into her opening, then thrusting balls deep in one move. She moves forward with a grunt, then pushes back against me. All concern for my brother, for my future, for whatever penance I still must pay to the universe, leaves my mind. There's only us, and this incredible heat. I bend over her and slide my arm around her front, caressing her soft belly, then dragging my hand lower to her slick, bare pussylips. Her clit is hard, and she lets out a needy moan when I stroke it.

"You're so beautiful like this," I murmur into her ear as I stroke in and out of her tight pussy. "In the fresh air. We should fuck outside every day."

"We do," she says with a laugh, then a moan as I shift my angle. "Yes, like that." I bring my other hand to her belly, and press. She lets out a long, low moan. "I'm close, Nico."

Just hearing her say that makes my balls tighten, knowing that when she squeezes around my shaft, I'll be lost. I thrust harder, press harder, and she shatters with a cry, contracting around me, squeezing me until my vision spots. I cry out driving into her, as deep as she'll take me, my come releasing in hot spurts, until I'm empty, and I've marked the inside of her. And in some primal, caveman part of my brain, I wish that we were making babies. The thought shocks me sober, the warm buzz of my orgasm dissipating. I pull out, and we clean ourselves up as best we can, knowing there's a shower in our future.

Alison cocks her head at me, concern flashing in her eyes. "Everything okay?"

"Yeah." I force a smile. "Everything's great."

"Okay, so you won't mind if I finish up on my own and I send you down to the bottom of the lot to mend a section of fence?"

"Wait, so you were just buttering me up for a job you know I hate?"

Her eyes twinkle. "Maybe. You saying it's too much for you?" She snaps her overalls back into place.

"I'm gonna spank your ass when we get into the shower," I call after her.

She wiggles said ass, and looks back over her shoulder with a saucy grin. "Promise?"

Declan finds me down at the fence, imagining exactly how I plan to punish Alison in the shower. "I need you to run this into town," he says brusquely, holding out a thick envelope.

"Something wrong with your legs?" He could have driven into town in the time it probably took him to hike down here.

"I'm waiting for delivery of the harvesting bins."

He's full of shit. I know for a fact they're not due to show up until tomorrow. And since when has he taken an interest in the daily runnings of the vineyard. But then I catch a glimpse of who the letter's addressed to- Emmaline Andersson. I know exactly what's going on, and I'm just enough of an asshole to capitalize on it. "Fine, sure. I'll take it. But it'll cost you."

"Anything."

I smother a laugh. He's fucking desperate to not go to town. "Dinner for two at French Laundry," I deadpan.

He blinks. Then blinks again. "That's a thousand bucks, easy."

I shrug and turn back to the fence. "Suit yourself." I give him thirty seconds before he buckles.

He caves in ten. "Okay, fine. But I want to know who your date is."

"Oh, she's not a date," I deny, although that's the furthest thing from the truth.

"Who is it, then?"

"Alison."

"Alison," he parrots, surprise flashing across his face.

Now, I'm pissed. "She's been working her ass off, and you've hardly noticed." He's been so depressed, he hasn't noticed the lines of tension around her eyes and mouth, the knots in her shoulders that no number of orgasms seem to relax.

"I've noticed," he backpedals. "And besides, I'm paying her a fortune."

I glare. "Can't you see she's exhausted? Or are you too wrapped up in your grief to notice?"

Declan sags, pinching the bridge of his nose. "Okay, fine. Take her to dinner. And tell her thanks."

God, is this the way I was when I was helping dad run things? A heartless fuck? *Yes,* the dark voice of my conscience answers. "Why don't you tell her that," I snap, vowing to do a better job of appreciating people.

"Fine, I will." He snaps back, muttering *asshole* under his breath.

His insult catches me by surprise, and I let out a laugh.

"Yep. I am, What're you gonna do about it?" I promise to drop the letter in the four o'clock mail, and finish repairing the fence.

I find Alison back in the tiny office at the far corner of the crushing pad. I pause in the doorway, watching her work. She hums under her breath as she taps at the keys, then leans forward to study something, hand drifting to the knot that won't leave her neck. She's pushing herself too hard. But I also get why she's doing it, and I wish there was more I could do to help.

"I'm taking you to dinner."

She squeaks and turns around, startled.

"French Laundry. Be ready at six." I turn and head for the trailer and the shower that's calling my name. Tonight, I'm going to show Alison just how special she is.

Chapter Twenty-Three

Alison

*T*he rest of the day crawls by. It doesn't help that I glance at the time every three-and-a-half minutes. French Laundry? People don't just go there on a whim. It takes weeks, usually months to get a reservation. How long has Nico been planning this?

My heart sinks. Maybe he already had reservations. But still, I reassure myself, he's taking *me*. He could have just canceled the reservations. So I let myself go back to thinking that yeah, *this is a really big deal*. And what am I going to wear? I immediately land on the coral colored vee neck wrap around dress I bought on a whim a few weeks ago when I binge purchased new panties and non-uniboob sports bras. Nico mentioned he wanted me to wear my hot pink ankle boots with a skirt, and this dress will work perfectly. *But what about shapewear?* Fuck. There's no denying, I'm... lumpy. I've got dimples on my thighs and ass, and gentle rolls on my belly. And while I can get away with leggings and long, colorful tunics, and jeans with a healthy percentage of spandex, there's no hiding those flaws under a body-skimming wrap dress without shapewear. I have just the thing, too- a pale pink pinup girl thing with a sheer bra and lace covering the spandex panels, but it's unwieldy. I smirk, Nico will just have to work for his treasure if he was serious about wrapping my ankles around his neck.

At four, I can't stand it anymore. I slam my laptop shut, just as my phone rings. Kimmie's picture lights up the screen. Talking to her will be just the distraction I need. "Hey sis," I answer brightly.

"You've been avoiding me," she accuses without even a 'how are you?'

"I'm doing great, actually. Thanks for asking."

She cuts right to the chase. "You're still with him, aren't you? That's why you've been avoiding me."

She's not wrong. "I promise, he's not like what he was. He's thoughtful, and he makes me laugh." And holy shit, the sex.

"He's bamboozled you. You're thinking with sex hormones. Have you thought about how he's going to react when you finally 'fess up? Because if you keep seeing him, you're going to have to."

I hate it when she goes all big-sister on me. I love it, too. "Why should I have to tell him? Nobody else knows."

"Katie-bug-"

"*Stop* calling me that."

"Okay, fine. But that's my point- your past is part of who you are. Do you honestly think you can hide that from someone you have a serious relationship with?"

"Tommy didn't know," I say stubbornly.

"Tommy was a shit who didn't deserve you."

"But that's not why I didn't tell him. Don't you understand, Kimmie? My life's not an open book the way yours is. I don't want *anyone* to know how or who I was, and I wish you'd all stop talking about it." My parents, at least, try not to speak of it much, but they won't remove the pictures of me from then. I can still hear the last conversation I had about that with my mom. *I love all of you sweetie, no matter what you used to look like. I'm proud of you. Always.* And I appreciate that, I do. But all I see is shame, pain, and profound unhappiness when I look at the younger version of myself, and I can't bear it.

"Okaaayyy," she answers dubiously. "I just don't want you to get hurt, honey."

"I won't. And it's not like this is forever," I rush to reassure her. "We both know this is just a thing." A thing I'm starting to wish won't have an end date. Because why would you end something with someone you love? For a second, my hopes rise. Maybe that's why he's bringing me to dinner someplace fancy? I know there's not a ring in my future, but French Laundry is the place where those kinds of discussions take place.

"If you're sure," she says, voice still filled with concern.

"I'm sure."

"Okay, and now I have some good news."

"Oh?"

"I'm being sent to LA for a six-month project starting the week before Thanksgiving."

I squeal into the phone. I haven't seen my sister in over a year. "I'll come down every weekend during the off-season," I promise. "We'll have so much fun. And I'll come down for Thanksgiving. We can do it at the beach." My mind fills with all the sisterly adventures we can take while she's stateside.

"I'll be home for two weeks before that visiting Mom, and Dad and Hami." Hami is my dad's mom, who's always lived with us, short for Halmoni, which I couldn't say as a kid, and so it morphed into Hami. Kimmie's always been her favorite. She was prettier and more obedient than I was. And she wasn't fat. But I've made peace with that now, for the most part.

"So why don't I plan to come home after the final harvest? We can have early Thanksgiving in Kansas City."

"I love it. Okay, keep me posted. And sis?"

"Be careful with your heart, please?"

"I am. I promise." I don't know what else to say. She needs to see how Nico's changed for herself.

I tuck my cellphone back in my pocket and head for the trailer. There, I shower and shave until I am smooth and soft all over. I apply my favorite rose-scented moisturizer, compliments of my sister, and take the time to paint both my fingers and toes. Painting my fingernails is an exercise in futility, the polish will chip the second I slide my hands into work gloves, but I'm going all out tonight. I select hot pink for my toes, and a pale pink for my nails. I straighten my hair so that it falls in a curtain down my back. I can honestly say, I've always liked my hair. Liked its color, the thickness, and how glossy it is. I lucked out in that department, getting more of Dad's genes. Kimmie's hair on the other hand, has a slight kink she's always battling with. And it's lighter than mine, thanks to Mom's Polish heritage.

I struggle into my shapewear, shimmying, grunting and tugging until it's firmly in place squeezing my softness into very structured lines. I preen in the mirror. I don't look half-bad, and the undergarment pulls the girls high, so I'll have a nice cleavage line going in the vee of my dress. I slip the dress over my head, adjust the waistband

and tie it in a nice bow so that the tails cascade down my left hip.

I resist looking in the mirror until I've put on my pink ankle boots. I gasp when I finally look. I'm not girly, I've never *been* girly. The only jewelry I own is compliments of Kimmie. But I have to admit, I look *goooooooood*. Like, kitty-cat meow, meow good. I do a circle, checking for lines, and also admiring the figure I see in the mirror. Still too chubby for my taste, but I'm coming to terms with that. And it hasn't been off-putting to Nico at all. I search my minimal jewelry collection and settle on a thick silver bracelet, and a pair of long skinny Swarovski crystal earrings.

I keep my makeup minimal, mascara, eyeliner, and a dark coral lipstick that matches my dress. I head to the living room to wait, and discover Nico waiting on the couch. With flowers. Wearing a suit. I have no idea where he managed to get a suit that has obviously been hand-tailored, but he wears it perfectly, with an air of James Bond, and my mind jumps ahead to the end of the evening when I can peel it off him, piece by piece.

He rises, eyes roving over me. "You. Look. Stunning."

I bask in his affection, warming to my toes. "Thank you," I murmur, giving him a turn so he can see all of me."

"You're incredible," he murmurs, pulling me in for a gentle kiss, then handing me the bouquet of pink peonies and roses.

"Wow, thank you," I say accepting them, popping up on my toes to kiss his jaw. "I guess this is a real date, huh?"

"You deserve it," he says with a burr in his throat, turning to take my mouth again. "I see you're wearing those shoes."

I flick my eyebrows at him. "Indeed. I look forward to wrapping them around your neck later."

The growl he lets out is feral, as he buries his face

against my neck, nipping at my collarbone. "And I can't wait to see your luscious pink lips wrapped around my cock," he mutters, pressing against me.

"We could skip dinner," I offer, eager to get to the best part of the night.

"Another time. Tonight, I want to wine you and dine you,"

"Before you sixty-nine me?" I tease.

He slaps me on the ass, grinning. "Put those flowers in water, and let's go."

"I've been meaning to ask," I start, as we approach the parking lot at the restaurant. "How long have you had reservations?"

Nico cuts the engine and turns, jaw tight. Butterflies launch in my belly. My question has offended him. "This afternoon. Dec owed me a favor, and I told him he could pay me by buying us dinner tonight."

I want to sink into the butter soft leather of Declan's car, which Nico insisted we drive down the mountain instead of my old Nissan. "Here?"

Nico nods once, pulse ticking at his temple. "Here."

"Oh," I whisper. "Wow."

His finger crooks under my jaw, turning my face to his. "You're worth it Alison."

I don't know how to respond to that except to nod and smile. Inside I feel like an overturned salt-shaker. I feel like things are spinning out of control. People will recognize Nico, just the way they did at the winemaker's happy hour. Out here, we're a couple. Up on the mountain, we're a delicious, secluded secret.

His mouth, when his lips graze mine, is tender. Reverent, even. And the butterflies in my belly swirl and dive in a wild, unified dance. The only thing I can hear is my heartbeat, thunking rapidly. "Come on, angel," he says when we break apart. "You're in for a treat."

It's everything I've dreamed of for a food experience. The food and wine are expertly prepared, and I have to pace myself or I'll be full, long before the last course arrives.

"Eat," Nico gestures with his fork. "You're leaving your plate half-full."

"I won't have room for dessert." Truth. Mostly.

"That's a sin," he says, diving after a piece of scallop on my plate. He stares at me hard. "And a lie. You barely eat, ever, hon."

It's on my lips to tell him, to begin letting out my truth piece by piece, when there's a commotion at the front of the restaurant. Declan walks in, an angry purple bruise squeezing an eye shut, trailed by another man looking equally worse for wear. I push back from the table. "Declan? What on earth?"

"Austin," Nico mutters rising. And the next word he utters turns my blood cold. "And Jason."

"What do you want?" Nico asks with quiet menace.

I've never heard Nico's voice like this. Filled with such anger, eyes cold.

Austin clears his throat. "We need to talk to you."

Nico shakes his head. "I'm busy."

"Now, Nico. It's important."

"Did somebody die?"

His questions are directed at Austin. He's not even looking at Jason, and I wonder how long it's been since he's seen his older brother, and what's going through his head.

Austin shakes his head. "No, but-"

"Then we're through here." Nico steps back in front of his chair. "Come up to the vineyard tomorrow."

"It's about the company," Austin says, stepping closer.

"And I wouldn't have interrupted your… soirée," he throws a glance my direction. "If it wasn't an emergency."

Heat flushes my face, and I wish the earth would swallow me. In Nico's world, people like me are expendable. A pleasant dinner companion to pass the time between doing 'important' things.

Nico gives me a tortured look, and I reach across to squeeze his hand. "It's okay. I can wait." I give him a crooked smile. "Let my food digest. I'll ask the server to hold the next course."

Nico runs a hand through his hair, looking between us, clearly warring with himself. "Okay." He nods, then maneuvers around the table to kiss my cheek. "I'll be back shortly."

I nod, and sit, watching him follow his brothers through the restaurant and out the door. Ten minutes turns to twenty, then forty. The server returns at an hour. "Miss? I'm sorry, the chef is asking if you're planning on finishing?"

My eyes prickle, and I pull in a shaky breath. "Yes, sure."

"Shall I bring both plates?"

My heart sinks. Surely he'll be back any minute? He wouldn't leave me here to explain, the receiver of pitying looks, and quiet comments behind my back. *But what if he's not coming back?* I don't know what's worse, me finishing alone, or me finishing alone with two plates at the table. I swallow. "Just one, thank you," I say barely above a whisper. If Nico comes back we can share his plate and he can tell me all about what happened with his brothers.

I don't taste the food that's presented. And with each course, I take fewer and fewer bites. It's a waste of the chef's talent and expensive food. By the time dessert is presented, I realize Nico's not coming back. A half-hysterical laugh threatens to escape, because I don't know whether to laugh or cry. Kimmie was right, leopards don't change their spots.

It's only after I've driven slowly up the mountain, wiped the makeup from my face, and struggled out of my shapewear and crawled under the covers that I see the text Nico sent hours ago.

I'm sorry. I have to go. I promise I'll make it up to you.

Chapter Twenty-Four

Nico

$\mathcal{I}$ follow my brothers out of the restaurant, stewing. This better be fucking good, because the look on Alison's face when she told me to go, punched me in the guts. All I want to do is get back to her and reassure her everything's okay. Better than okay. We stop by a stand of trees on the far side of the lot. "If you've come to get the band back together, I'm a firm no."

Austin smiles wryly and reaches into a messenger bag. I don't look at Jason. He's fucking dead to me until further notice. "Maybe this will change your mind." He hands me a stack of papers.

"What in the hell is this?"

"A paper trail of how Dad's board has been fleecing him for years."

I'm not at all surprised. I suspected as much and tried to take him aside two years ago, but he wouldn't hear of it, and stupidly, I didn't want to piss him off further, so I dropped it, figuring I'd fire the board when I was crowned new CEO. "And?"

Austin smiles grimly. "It's time to stage a family coup."

I hand him back the papers. "Good luck with that. Now if you'll excuse me, I've got a dinner date."

"Wait," Jason utters, arms folded across his chest.

I spin, the scab ripping off the old wound. "And why the *fuck* are you even here?" I ask, jabbing a finger at his chest.

"Says the guy who married *my* fiancé."

The old anger bubbles up and takes over. "You wanna talk about that? Assfuck? Go ahead. Let's talk about the matching scars we all sport. Shall we start there?"

Jason stares at me implacably, unfazed by my outburst, which only serves to rile me up more.

"Or shall we start with the puppy? The bruises we hid from Mom and Dad? Or the nightmares? You're a fucking twisted fuck, you know that?"

"I'm sorry."

"All I wanted to do was hurt you, to make you feel-*what'd you say?*" His words sink in, stopping my tirade. But then I promptly start up again. "And now you think this is all going to go away with a simple I'm sorry? Fuck. You." I jab his chest, voice rising. I don't give a shit if the patrons in the parking lot can hear me. I'm fucking airing my laundry.

"Hear him out, Nico." Austin pleads.

"Shut-up. He doesn't deserve shit after what he's done to us."

Jason opens his hands. "You're right. I was a shit. Worse. I was mean, and very, very fucked-up. I had a lot of time to think when I was at Walter Reed recovering."

"But you were home after that and you didn't say shit."

"And why would I? You rubbed my nose in your marriage every day."

He has a point. I was a dick about that, and I enjoyed every second of my assholery, until it caught up with me. "And you can see how well it worked out for me."

Jason gives me a tight smile.

"I'm not ready to forgive you."

Jason nods his understanding. "I'm not asking for that. But Millie... she's on..." He shakes his head. "Fuck, man. I'm going to be a father, and all I can think about is how I would fucking wring the neck of someone who did that to my kids. What I did."

"And he's getting help," Austin chimes in.

I raise my eyebrows, looking to Jason for confirmation. He nods. "Yeah. There's a shrink in town that works with a lot of military cases. Head cases like me."

"Have you talked to Dec?"

Austin nods. "He's taking a few days. You should too. Look over the paperwork. I want to go to Dad with a plan."

"And that is?"

"You take your rightful place as CEO, I take over as CFO, Declan takes care of acquisitions."

"And what about assfuck, here?" I tip my head toward Jason. I'm so far from ready to kiss and make up.

"I relinquished my shares when I left for Kansas. I'm not reclaiming them."

"What about our trust-funds?"

Austin smiles darkly. "They'll be restored. Immediately."

So my days of being a pauper will be over. There are worse fates. I wonder what Alison would say about all this.

We've talked a lot about Jason, about my childhood. She'd tell me to find a way to move forward. And for her I would, but not without taking my shot, first. I turn to Jason. "I want to beat the shit out of you."

The corner of his mouth kicks up. "Stealing my fiancé wasn't enough?"

"Not even close," I growl.

He steps back, opening himself. "Take your shot. What's another few bruises?"

I wind up, ready to unleash the punch I've been imagining taking since I was a kid. Then I drop my arm, suspicious. This has got to be some kind of a setup. "Why are you doing this?"

"The truth?" Jason asks.

I roll my eyes. "No. How about a bullshit sandwich?"

Behind me, Austin chuckles.

Jason shrugs. "Millie. And her dad. Mostly Millie. She sees me, and somehow she still loves me. She makes me-"

"Want to be a better man," I finish for him, thinking of Alison waiting for me inside. I can't argue with that. And I only hope that if someone confronted me with any of my past shittiness, that they could understand I want to be a better man, too. I look down at the papers in my hand. "I'm in."

"You sure? It's a big decision," Austin cautions. "If you're serious, you should come back to the hotel and I can bring you up to speed."

"What's our time frame?" I ask, surprised at how easy it is to step back into CEO mode.

"ASAP. We're hemorrhaging cash. The sooner we stop it, the better."

"What's that going to take?"

"I had my lawyer draw up agreements of rolls and

responsibilities. Under the board rules, we need to get dad to call an emergency meeting. Between the three of us and Dad, we have enough shares to fire the board and start over."

"Do you have new board members in mind?"

Austin nods, excitement lighting his eyes. "I do. And if you can get away, we can discuss it all. I'd like to go to dad as soon as Dec signs on."

I look back at the restaurant, my plans for the evening gone up in smoke. As much as I want to go back in there and pick up where we left off, I have an obligation to the family business. It's been my destiny, my dream, and Alison would want me to go. I think of our business conversations, maybe this is a chance for Case Family Wineries to turn over a new leaf, too.

I shoot Alison a text, not wanting to make more of a scene than we already did. *I'm sorry. I have to go. I promise I'll make it up to you.*

"One more thing," Austin cautions. "If you take over, I'm not gonna be in Napa full-time."

"Why not?" Then I see his answer written all over his face. "Let me guess. You've gone and fallen for someone."

His goofy grin says it all.

I roll my eyes. "Jesus, fuck. What in the hell is in the water out there in Kansas?"

It's dawn when I crawl into bed and gather Alison in my arms. "I'm sorry, sweetheart. I promise I'll take you there again, and I won't tell anyone where I am." She nuzzles her head into my shoulder and as I stroke her hair, I realize she's crying. My stomach hollows. Fuck me, I made her cry. "Oh, baby, please don't cry. Give me a chance to explain."

Her shoulders shake harder, but she nods, and pushes up to sitting, tucking the sheets under her arms.

It concerns me, that she's not saying anything, she's just staring at me with hurt in her eyes. I clear my throat, unsure where to start, because I realize in her mind, maybe sorting out my family's business isn't reason enough to ditch your date. "So last May, at Jason's wedding, my dad gave the three of us- me, Austin, and Dec, an ultimatum. He froze our trust funds, and told us we had to take a more active interest in the family business in order to unfreeze them. I've already been actively involved in the business, so I did what any self-respecting son would do in that case- I told him to fuck the hell off."

She snorts and her mouth twitches.

"Once Veronica realized the family faucet was turned off, she kicked me out, and you know the rest of that story."

She nods her head, still not talking.

My stomach roils. I don't want to lose her over this. "I landed at my accountant's house because I didn't want to take a handout from Dec, but he turned out to be as crooked as Ronnie, so I fired him and landed... here." I reach out and trace a finger over her collarbone. "And it's the best damned thing that ever happened to me."

She shuts her eyes, but a tear squeezes out the corner and runs down her cheek.

Every tear is like a knife stabbing into my chest. I cup her face. "I mean it, angel. You're the best thing that has ever happened to me." She sniffs loudly and lets out a little half-sob. But it's her tentative smile that arrows straight into my heart. "I love you Ali. Don't ever doubt that." Even though things are about to get really complicated. "When Austin showed up today- *yesterday* with Jason, I wanted to rip his face off, or worse. But I thought about all the conversations we've had about picking yourself up and moving on, and-and, while I don't want to be his friend, and I'm not sure I've forgiven him, I think we've at least reached an understanding."

"I'm happy for you," she murmurs.

"The worst part? It turns out, Jason had planned to call off their engagement when he got home from his deployment. So all that time I thought I was hurting him- he didn't care. I was only hurting myself."

She lets out a wry laugh. "That's karma for you."

"I hope I'm done with karmic retribution."

"So what else happened?"

The tightness in my chest eases, now that she's talking. "Austin came out for a visit sometime late July, to scout some growers, and discovered that the company has been leaking dollar bills right into the pockets of the board members for years. He built a solid paper trail and if Declan signs on, he's going to take it to Dad and force him to retire. I'll become CEO, and we'll fire the current board."

Alison blows out a long breath. "Wow. Just. *Wow.*"

"I'm still trying to wrap my head around it."

"What's your timeframe?"

"ASAP. We need to stop the bleeding and work on some damage control right away. Harvest has already started, so we're going to have to wait for major changes until December."

"So, I guess that means you'll be moving back to Napa." She frames it as a statement.

I nod, hating every second of what's coming. This is the part I've been dreading. "Yeah. I'm going to need to be down at headquarters, so it makes sense. But it's only what? Forty minutes? That's nothing. And I can come up on the weekends."

"Won't that look suspicious to Declan?"

"I don't care," I growl, pulling her in for a kiss. "Why shouldn't the whole world know I love you?" I say with more confidence than I feel. This is just a bump, and we'll figure it out. I know it.

Chapter Twenty-Five

Alison

I accept Nico's hand as I make my way down the steps from the private jet to the tarmac. We've spent the morning flying cross-country to Kansas City. Well, actually the pilots did that. Nico and I were tangled up in the king-sized bedroom at the back of the plane. I never imagined myself becoming a member of the mile-high club once, let alone four times.

I'm relaxed enough, I'm tempted to invite Nico to our Not-Thanksgiving dinner. But only tempted, because I'm pretty sure all hell would break loose if I brought Nico home to meet my family. The problem is, every excuse I've manufactured has fallen on deaf ears.

"So you're taking me home to meet your parents, right?" He says, kissing the back of my hand that's entwined in his. "I want to see where you grew up."

"Believe me, I'm saving you from a third-degree grilling that may involve instruments of torture."

He stops and pulls me close, tucking a flyaway strand of hair behind my ear. "If that's what I have to go through to get your family's approval, then so be it."

I'm pretty sure butterflies vacated my stomach somewhere over Utah. They've been replaced by pinballs. I can hardly stand it. "Okay, so what if we run by and I introduce you, and then we get settled in the hotel, and I'll go back for dinner with my sister?" He's not going to let up, I can see the determined look in his eye.

He cups my face, staring right into my soul. "What are you afraid of?"

"Everything," I blurt.

"I promise I'll be on my best behavior. We can stop and I'll bring flowers along with the wine."

He's referring to the bottles of Madame M Chardonnay and Redwood Reserve, the surprise barrels we bottled. I wish more than anything I could say I was responsible for making them, but the only credit I get is sharing them with the world. But my parents will be proud nonetheless. And next year, I'll be able to present them with a bottle of wine that's entirely mine.

"I… it's just the last man I brought home was my ex-husband." Lame excuse, and not at all why I'm terrified, but it's the truth. At least part of it.

He gives me a sympathetic nod. "So… you don't want to jinx us?"

"I, no, *what?*" I narrow my eyes. "What are you saying, Nico?" Kangaroos replace the pinballs in my stomach.

"Well, we are here for a wedding," he starts.

"Your brother's. And Austin's going to be a father in the spring."

"And your point is?"

He smirks.

"Are you fucking with me?" I gently punch him in the

shoulder. "You're fucking with me, and I'm gonna kick your ass."

"Not before I spank yours," he teases, and a jolt of heat goes straight to my pussy. I like it when he spanks me.

"Seriously," he drops a kiss on my head. "I want to meet your family and assure them of my good intentions."

"Whatever that's supposed to mean." I snark, mind racing at how I'm going to spin this with my family.

It's only a fifteen-minute drive from the downtown airport to the Brookside neighborhood where I spent the remainder of my high school years. My heart beats faster at every stoplight. By the time we roll to a stop in front of the house, I'm pretty sure I'm going to go into cardiac arrest. Or have a stroke. My heart is beating so fast, my teeth start to chatter.

Nico reaches across the console and grabs my hand. "Hey. Are you okay?"

I nod quickly. "Just nervous."

He hops out of the car, grabs the gift bag from the back seat, and walks around front, fingers dragging across the hood, and opens my door, extending me a hand to help me out. Always the gentleman, and a good thing too, because I can see my Hami peeking through the curtains. She's the least of my worries. I clutch my purse so hard my knuckles turn white.

He places his hand on the small of my back and stays by my side as we head up the walk to the porch. My sister is out the door before we hit the top step, catching me up in a hug so tight, it brings tears to my eyes. She steps back, eyes shining. "Look at you." There's so much emotion in her voice, so much love and pride, it hurts.

I clear my throat. "Ah, Kimmie. This is Nico. Nico, meet my sister Kimmie."

She extends her hand, demeanor twenty-degrees cooler. "A pleasure, I've heard so much about you."

Nico side eyes me. I shrug. "Sister talk," I murmur.

My parents huddle in the doorway, waiting to cover me with hugs, and which they do as soon as Kimmie lets me go. I steal a glance at Nico, who seems calm, waiting patiently for the greetings to finish. "Mom, Dad... this is Nicholas Case." I stumble over his name, because even though I'm sure Kimmie has mentioned something, this is the first time they're coming face to face with the person who once caused me so much pain."

There's an awful, awkward moment, when both my parents look shocked, then angry, and then it's gone. Their smiles are in place, and they're offering their hands in welcome. "Come, in. Welcome to our home," my father says in his stilted accent. Even after living here more than thirty-five years, he still speaks with a foreign lilt.

My mother would die of mortification before she was inhospitable. "Nicholas, it's such a pleasure to meet one of Ali's..." she shoots me a questioning glance. "Friends." I nod, not wanting to explain all the details to them just yet.

I slip off my shoes, placing them on the rug.

Nico follows suit without blinking an eye, smile at the ready. "Please, call me Nico. And here, these are for you." He offers her the bag. "We wanted to bring you something from the vineyard."

"They're not mine," I'm quick to point out. "But it will give you an idea of what I'll be making."

She gives my cheek a pat. "Oh sweetie pie. We're so proud of you. You know that. Well, quit standing and letting the cold air in. Come inside. Hami's waiting to greet you."

"Hami," I grin, then give her the greeting I was trained

to give her from the time I could talk. "*Annyeong halmeoni,*" I say with a bow.

She nods with a smile. My dad rattles something off to her in Korean, and her eyes flick to Nico.

Nico bows too, repeating my words with a much better accent. "*Annyeong halmeoni.*"

It shouldn't surprise me he knows Korean pleasantries. He's probably entertained clients from all over the world, and knows how to say hello in twenty-three languages. But it does. And it warms my heart to see Hami light up. At least one person besides me is sold on him. Then I spy a picture of me and Kimmie from my thirteenth birthday party standing in a corner of the bookshelf. "Kimmie, can you show Nico where the kitchen is?" I flick my eyes at the picture.

She flicks her eyes back at me, giving me one of those sisterly *what the fuck do you think you're doing* looks.

I beg with my eyes. In the meantime, Nico's looking back and forth between us with an amused smile. "Mrs. Walker, I'd love to see your home."

The air goes out of the room as my parents exchange awkward glances. Fuck. *Fuckfuckfuck.* I give Nico an apologetic smile. "Ahh, it's Park. I, ahh… never bothered to change my name back after my divorce." I think I might puke. Nico's been in the house less than five minutes, and without even trying, he's stepped in the pile of shit that is my former life.

My mother comes to the rescue. "No worries, hon. Ali's always done things a little differently."

Understatement of the year. Nico's looking at me, but I can't read him. He's schooled his features, and I wonder if I'm going to miss out on my spanking later. Then he flashes me a wicked smile. "She does, doesn't she?"

Oh hell yes, we are *so* going to the kinky place tonight.

My mother ushers him into the kitchen, and as soon as he's out of sight, I hurry to the photo and drop it into my purse.

"*What* are you doing?" Kimmie hisses. "Are you insane? You can't erase yourself from this house."

"Oh hell, yes I can, and you're going to help me."

She crosses her arms. "Oh no, I'm not. If you're serious enough, which God help me, I don't understand, to bring him to the house, you need to come clean."

"Now is not the time to pull out the big sister routine," I say tersely, as I scan the bookshelves for other evidence of my old life.

She follows me to the second bookshelf, where I pull off a picture of the two of us when I was four and Kimmie was ten, standing in our swimsuits on the front lawn of our apartment in Palo Alto, playing with the garden hose. That one can stay. I return the photo to its spot. It's the teenage and college ones that have to go. I scan the room, double checking the corners for frames, and I spy the family photo album on the bottom shelf of the coffee table.

I make a beeline for it and Kimmie follows. "No one is going to get out the family photo album."

"You don't know mom." I turn and look at her, panic making my fingers tingle. "Please, Kimmie? Just this once. I swear I'll tell him. I just need more… time. It's been so crazy, and now with Declan getting married tomorrow. Please?"

Her eyes fill with pity. I hate it. I hate that my sister feels sorry for me, but on this point, she doesn't understand. She's been beautiful and perfect her whole life. She has nothing to be ashamed of. She shuts her eyes with a grimace. "Give me the album. I'll stash it in my suitcase."

"Check the hall photos?" I call behind her.

She'll do it. She's always been on my side. And today, especially, I'm so grateful.

My mom and Nico return a moment later. "I can't wait for Not-Thanksgiving," Nico says, eyes twinkling. "Is it time to eat yet?"

"Don't say I didn't try to warn you," I whisper as we head into the dining room.

Not-Thanksgiving is not for the faint of heart, or for those with a delicate constitution. It's what happens when you grow up in a Polish Korean house. Not-Thanksgiving consists of pierogies, kapusto, kimchi, and jap chae, to name a few. But by the time we all toss our napkins on the table two hours later, the mood is decidedly less strained. Until Nico speaks up. "This has been great tonight." He reaches for my hand. "I've loved seeing where Ali grew up."

The silence immediately becomes awkward, and my dad, always a stickler for precision says "Oh, she didn't grow up here."

"Oh?"

"Both the girls were born when I was at Stanford."

"No kidding?" Nico's voice turns excited. "Class of '12. We'll have to trade stories." Nico turns to me. "You've been holding out on me. I didn't know you were a California girl."

Oh, I am going to hell for my lies. I know it. Or some kind of dragon universe where there's lots of fire. "We moved here when I was..." I search for something mostly truthful, because I can*not* lie in front of my dad. "Younger. And then I attended Cornell for college, but you already knew that," I say, pushing the conversation ahead. "Who's ready for dessert?"

Chapter Twenty-Six

Nico

*W*e get a late start from Kansas City... for obvious reasons, but the last several weeks have been brutal between bringing myself up to speed as Case Family Wineries new CEO, bringing in two harvests, and planning the opening release party for Fieldstone Winery.

The lines of exhaustion around Ali's eyes are more pronounced, and I insisted we make a slow morning of it. Ali covers a yawn as we speed down the highway toward Prairie, Kansas where Dec and Emmaline are getting married later today. "I could get used to room service," she says with a smile.

"You hardly touched your eggs," I remind her. "I think half the reason you're so tired is that you don't eat enough." This has been an ongoing argument for us, and so far, one I can't win.

"I had some," she says with a defensive note in her

voice. "And fruit. And I promise you, I'll eat when I'm hungry again. Besides, it's not like I'm starving." She scowls into her lap.

"Alison." I reach for her thigh, stroking up. "I think you're perfect the way you are."

The smile on her face says she doesn't believe it. "I think you're crazy."

"Yes. I am. For you, angel."

She laughs and shakes her head, then gives me a look filled with such hope and simultaneous doubt that my heart squeezes tight.

"Don't look at me that way," I say, voice rough. "I mean it, Alison. I love you."

"I know. And I love you, too."

"But?" I feel like there's a caveat in her statement. I've felt it for weeks- ever since I agreed to take over as CEO, but I haven't been able to tease it out, yet.

"No buts. Just, I love you too." She smiles, and this time it reaches her eyes.

"So, I've been thinking."

"Don't tell me you've come up for another name for the Cabernet. We haven't even barreled it yet."

I chuckle. It turns out neither of us is good at naming wine. Ali's sister Kimmie, came up with the name Redwood Reserve for the estate wine we just released. "No, nothing that ambitious." I take a breath. "I think you should move down to Napa with me." I've been thinking about this ever since I relocated down the mountain for the sake of the business. I hate sleeping apart from her, I miss our daily connection. She doesn't say anything, so I continue. "I've been staying at my old apartment on the estate, but there's no reason why we couldn't get a house that was a quick drive away."

"For you."

"Pardon?"

"A quick drive away for you. What about for me? I don't want to commute."

"But it's not that far."

"I'm happy where I am, Nico. I love being up at the winery. I love my morning jogs, I love the solitude and the peace up there."

"But you're living in a foreman's trailer."

"So? You never complained about it when you stayed there."

"Because it was temporary."

"It is for me, too."

"I don't follow."

She shifts in her seat, turning her body my direction. "I have a plan to buy out Declan. Part of my contract with him was right of first refusal should he ever sell."

"But he won't, now that it's part of the family conglomerate."

"What?" Her eyes go wide and she shakes her head. "You're wrong. That property is solely in Declan's name, not your family's business. If he's selling it to you, he's selling it to *me* first." She glares, quivering with outrage.

"I don't see why you're upset. You'd still be the winemaker."

"Because I want my own place," she shouts, voice amplified in the small space of the rental car. "Don't you see? I don't want my success because I'm riding your coattails. I want it on my own merits."

I'm thoroughly confused. "But the wine is still your own. Think of the family business as a safety net in leaner years."

She crosses her arms, mouth thinned to a narrow line. "No."

"You're just being stubborn." I flex my hands on the

steering wheel, trying to keep my growing frustration in check. This is the first time we've spent significant alone-time together in weeks, and I don't want to argue. I want to reacquaint myself with every dip and crevice on her body, going on walks, sharing ideas.

"I'm being stubborn," she repeats, incredulous. Her voice rises again. "I'm being stubborn? You're the one who left the day you agreed to be CEO without a backward glance. You're the one who could work anywhere, and you won't work on the mountain."

"Because the offices are in Napa. And the trailer is too small for both of us to work there."

She glares at me. "Then figure it out, Mr. Genius CEO."

"I'm trying to, angel, in case you didn't notice," I grit out, tempted to pull over and kiss some sense into her. "Let me spell it out for you. I love you. I miss you. I don't like being apart from you. I *want* to figure out a solution. Are we clear?"

"Yes," comes her quiet reply.

I pinch my forehead, wishing that was all it took to get rid of the disappointment that's filled my chest. "Can we table this until we get home? I want to enjoy this weekend with you."

"Sure," she says with a nod.

———

I lean against the doorjamb watching Alison roll on a pair of lace-topped thigh highs. "You're going to leave those on when you finally wrap those pink boots around my neck, right?" Two pink streaks flame to life on her cheeks. I love making her blush, tossing dirty compliments her direction until she giggles and begs me to stop.

"You might want to do it now, before I struggle into my foundational undergarment." She says primly, covering her thighs with the barely-there pink satin robe she loves to wear.

"Foundational undergarment," I scoff. "Who in the fuck named that?"

She lifts a finely arched brow. "Our grandmothers used to call them girdles."

"Why wear it at all?" I'm purely selfish, of course. I want easy access to the parts of her I love most. "I love your curves."

"Not when they're lumpy."

"You're not lumpy in your robe," I point out, coming to where she's perched on the bed, so I can draw a finger down the vee of her neckline. She slaps my hand away with a giggle.

"Well, maybe next time. I want to look nice for the wedding."

I drop to my knees and insert myself between her legs, cheek caressing her inner thigh. I turn my head to kiss and lick the soft skin above the tops of her stockings until she sighs and lets her legs fall open further. "We have to go soon," she cautions.

Right now, I don't care if we're late, or if we miss Dec's wedding entirely. "Two minutes," I rumble against the outside of her smooth pussy. I've timed it, I can get her off in two minutes.

"You're already dressed."

"This is about you."

"Nico," she begs with a needy moan.

I take a long lick through her wet seam. We could spend the rest of our lives in bed and it wouldn't be enough.

"Are you sure?" I tease, licking through her folds again. I don't want to stop.

"No," she says on a sigh. "But I'm nervous." Her confession is enough to pull me away. I rise and land on the bed next to her, wiping my mouth with the back of my hand. She watches me hungrily. "You're so sexy when you do that."

She's deflecting. "Why are you nervous, sweetheart?"

She looks tortured. "I-I have a lot of social anxiety around parties."

"But you were great at the wine release."

"That was different. I was the winemaker then. I wasn't... me. Know what I mean?"

I do. "I promise I won't leave your side, if that's what you want. Danny will be there, too."

"But what if, what if..." she shakes her head with a sigh. "Never mind. It's silly. Old demons talking." She forces a smile. "I'm the new hotness, right?"

The affirmations that she hid in the drawer when I first arrived have slowly, one-by-one, returned to the mirror, and I'm touched she feels safe enough to refer to them. "You *are* the hotness, angel," I correct, covering her temple and cheek with kisses. "Now, if you're serious about not being late to the wedding. Hurry your sweet ass up, and know that as soon as we get back here after the reception, I'm peeling off that pretty pink dress-"

"Coral. It's coral."

"I don't care what color it is, I'm peeling it off you, and cutting off the what'd you call it?"

She smirks. "Foundational undergarment. But I'm not letting you cut it off. I paid good money for this."

"I'll replace it," I growl. "I'm cutting you out of it, and then you're wrapping those fuck-me hot boots around me while I make you scream my name."

She breaks into a smile that heats me straight to my balls. "Deal."

———————

Declan's pulled out all the stops for the wedding reception, which takes place at Jason's new vineyard. Gas heat lamps have been placed at intervals around the stone patio keeping the cold November air at bay. But I don't need a heat lamp to stay warm when Alison is dancing in my arms. My stomach growls loudly just as the band takes a break.

"Hungry?" Alison asks.

"Mostly for you," I say into her ear. "But we need sustenance. Let's go take a look at the buffet."

It's a true smorgasbord, with offerings from all of Emmaline's favorite restaurants. "Ooh, look at that ravioli," Alison coos, taking four, along with a small spoonful of caprese salad.

"I didn't know you liked Italian."

She crooks her head. "Why wouldn't I? I like everything."

I run a finger down the bridge of her nose. "Because I happen to know a great Italian restaurant in St. Helena I'd love to take you to."

"I think I'm free next weekend," she offers. "The Cabernet will be fermenting until after Thanksgiving, at least."

"It's a date," I say as we make our way to a set of low couches ringing a fire pit. Jason has brought his very pregnant wife Millie, out to a chaise so she can join us even though she's on bedrest. We're slowly patching things up. It's going to take work, but I can see how he's changed by the way he looks at Millie, the way he strokes her belly with a look of adoration and wonder. She- and this baby, are his world. I sneak a look at Alison and understand how he feels. All too easily, I can imagine making babies with Alison. I'm not even sure if she wants children. I tuck that thought away for later.

Austin and his girlfriend Macey- also expecting- have joined us, along with her red-headed daughter. Austin is smitten with her, pulling her onto his knee and bouncing her until she giggles. To my right, Danny and his girlfriend Roxi are squeezed into an oversized chair. Alison's thigh is pressed against mine, and it will have to suffice until we can make our excuses and walk back across the road to the hunting lodge that Jason's neighbors the Sinclaires run. "This must be where all the cool people sit," teases Declan as he joins us, arm wrapped around his bride.

Jason motions to the empty seat. "Join us."

Declan pulls Emmaline onto his lap and Jason raises his glass. "I think this might be the first time the four of us have been together without a brawl."

"Ya think?" Austin drawls, casting a sidelong glance at Macey.

Jason clears his throat. "It means a lot to me, to us-" He glances over to Millie who's reclining in the chaise next to him. "To be able to do this for you, Dec."

Dec nods.

Jason looks around the circle, meeting each of our eyes. "I know we still have a long way to go, but I'm grateful we're together tonight, and I'm looking forward to more gatherings like this."

I take Alison's hand and give it a squeeze, chest squeezing tight.

"It does feel like we've all turned over a new leaf," Austin adds, grinning stupidly at Macey, and then the rest of us.

I raise my glass, swallowing away the lump in my throat. "Here's to new beginnings, to fresh starts."

To my left someone slow claps, and an acid voice I hoped to never hear again turns my blood to ice. "Well, well. Isn't this sweet? All of you Cases making fresh starts. How long did you wait to start over, Nico? A week? A day?" asks my ex-wife, Veronica.

Chapter Twenty-Seven

Nico

I stand, gut clenching. Whatever she's here for, it's not good. "What are you doing here Veronica?"

She gives me a feral smile, and I wonder- seriously wonder- what I ever saw in her. There's no beauty there. Just nastiness. "Well, of course, I had to come give the happy couple my congratulations. And all these babies... how very sweet."

I stare at her, and make a quick count backward, realizing she should be showing too. But she's not. "I thought you were pregnant."

A pained expression crosses her face. "Well, yes. Sadly it seems I can't carry children."

She doesn't look sad at all. And I wonder, not for the first time, if she was ever pregnant at all, all those years ago. Millie's and Macey's hands fly to their bellies with murmured apologies.

Jason rises. "Whatever you have to say, say it," he grits. "You're not welcome at this party."

She turns to me, eyes big and soft. "I was hoping we could talk." Her voice is saccharine sweet, and the hackles on my neck rise up.

I shake my head. "Whatever you want to say, you can say to all of us."

She looks around the circle, eyes lighting on Danny and Roxi. "Ooh, you're not a Case. Who *are* you?"

"An honorary Case," Declan answers. "Say your peace, Ronnie and then I'm going to invite you to leave."

Her red-painted mouth pulls into a frown. "Fine," she snaps. "If that's how you want it." She turns to me, making puppy eyes. "I've been thinking, Nico, about what we had-"

Oh hell no, she's not going there. I cut her off. "About which part? The part where you cheated on me? Or the part where you ruined me?"

Her eyes narrow. "You don't look too ruined to me."

"That's why you're here, isn't it? That's why you've been calling Declan. Did your Senator figure out your game and give you the boot?" I shrug. "Sucks to be you."

Beside me, Alison gasps. Ronnie must have heard her too, because she fixes her attention on Alison. "Oh no, Nico. It sucks to be *you*. See, I did some digging on your rebound girlfriend here. Actually, Lara was the one who figured it out. Your chubby little winemaker isn't who you think she is."

I step forward, hand pulling into a fist. I force it open. "Shut your filthy mouth," I say with as much threat as I can muster.

Veronica laughs maniacally. "Don't you want to know? It really is rich." She turns an icy glare to Alison. "Isn't it, *Katie?*"

I turn. All the color is drained from Alison's face. She's still as a statue, hands fisted in her lap. I swing back to Veronica. "What in the hell are you talking about?"

"This." She pulls a folded piece of paper from her purse and hands it to me. It's from a yearbook and a face is circled in black marker. "I don't know who Alison Walker is, but *she's* Katie Park." Veronica points at Ali. "You've been fucking Katie the Cow."

Alison

Nine pairs of eyes swivel my direction- the women in shock, the men, eyes narrowed. They remember. I can see they remember. *Blubberball, Landwhale,* the mooing sounds, the taunts that ended in the entire class laughing at my expense. The one dance I attended where everyone did the new dance move- the whale. My body flushes hot, then goes ice-cold. So cold, I have to clench my teeth to keep them from chattering.

Nico looks from me to the paper with my three-hundred-plus-pound face, and back again, shock slowly turning to hurt, and then anger. "It's true, isn't it?" He crumples the paper in his fist. "What kind of game are you playing Ali?"

"Katie," Veronica corrects.

I open my mouth, but no sound comes out. I hear Kimmie's voice ringing in my ears. *You have to tell him.* I don't know where to start. "I-I can explain."

"You damn well better," he bites. "All those nights talking about forgiveness, and you've been holding out on me this whole time? Was this some kind of a sick revenge plot? Come back as someone else and kick me in the balls at the earliest opportunity?"

"It's not like that," I say, finding my voice again. "I swear."

He shakes his head. "Jesus. This is the kind of thing that shows up on Dr. Phil."

"*Nico,*" Jason calls from across the ring. "Calm down."

"I will not calm down. No fucking way." He turns to Danny. "Did you know about this? And knowingly set up my brother with a liar?"

"I am not a liar," I shout, leaping to my feet. Except I am. I am a total fucking liar. I've been living a lie since I was sixteen. "I'm *not.*" My voice catches.

Nico stalks back to me. "Then what are you? Katie?"

"Don't call me that," I say low and hard fighting to keep the tears from my voice.

"Then who are you?" he shouts. "Who the *fuck* did I fall in love with?"

I can't see through my tears, although I'm aware that others are also on their feet. I reach for him, my hand landing on his arm. "Please, Nico, let me explain."

He shrugs me off. "No. Not now. Just… go."

My stomach turns. I'm going to be sick, and that would be the worst humiliation. I stifle a sob and flee. I reach the edge of the parking lot before I retch in the bushes. Fucking Veronica and her sister Lara. Of my regular tormentors, Lara was the worst. I'm not sure how, but I manage to get back to the hunting lodge without turning an ankle. I quickly pack my bag, and wipe Nico's keys off the dresser. He can figure out how to get himself home.

Miraculously, I make it home without getting lost and without hitting a deer. I let myself into the house long after midnight, leave my shoes at the door, and stumble down the hall to Kimmie's room. "What is it?" she asks as I crawl into bed with her. "Oh honey, what happened?" She pulls me into her arms as the tears come.

"You were right." I sob. "You were right about everything."

Chapter Twenty-Eight

Nico

*F*our pairs of hands descend on me and haul me into the kitchen. Jason is the first to get in my face. "You want to tell me what in *fuck's sake* that shit was out there?"

"Don't start with me, asshole," I snap, the old anger quickly surfacing.

"You might be almost as tall as I am, but I can still kick your ass," he returns.

"I swear, I don't care what the fuck her name is, if you've cost me my winemaker, I'm ripping your balls off," Declan piles on.

"I told you to keep your pants zipped around her, assfuck," Danny adds.

Behind me, Austin laughs. I turn to glare, and he's bent over, clutching his side. "You fucked up big-time, dude. Tantrums like that are for pussies."

"Fuck you." My outburst just makes Austin laugh harder.

"Do you remember her? Katie?"

He shrugs. "Yeah, vaguely. I remember there was a fat girl a lot of people picked on."

"I remember her. Lara hated her. Probably because she was super smart, and Lara hated anyone who diverted attention from her."

"Just like her older sister," Jason adds wryly. "They're a fucking pair."

I go on, feeling sicker as the memories become clearer. "I think I had three or four classes with her- calc, chemistry, and for sure AP English. We were assholes. We cracked ourselves up coming up with new nicknames. It was more about one-upping each other and less about her. I just don't understand why she would lie to me."

"Jeezus, for a CEO, you're fucking obtuse," Austin chides. "How would you have felt if you'd been forced to work with Jason before… things were different?"

"Fuck," Declan mutters under his breath. "That was all my fault. I'm surprised she didn't quit on the spot." Declan turns to me. "You fucking better make this right, because I don't want to lose her."

I want to hang on to my hurt at her betrayal, my hurt that she didn't trust me enough to come clean at the get-go, but did I even give her a reason to trust me? Yes. Plenty.

Karma. The dark voice of my conscience cackles. And all the times she started to broach the subject come to my mind. The night of the winemaker's meeting, at the French Laundry just before Austin and Jason showed up. The hints that were plain as day that I just didn't see- the body dysmorphia, the conversations about forgiveness, even tonight when she mentioned how parties made her nervous. And fucking Veronica had to go reinforce that one. No wonder she wants to hide out on the top of Mt. Veeder and make wine where no one will bother her.

I turn to my brothers. "How could she really love me, when she's known all along what I did? What I was a part of?"

"I can answer that," says Millie, followed by Macey and Emmaline.

"You're supposed to be off your feet," growls Jason, worry crossing his face.

"You hush. You know as well as I do the doctor said I could come downstairs for a snack." Millie opens the fridge and pulls out a carton of soy milk. "So I'm having a snack. Oh, and Macey made sure Veronica left," she says while pouring herself a glass. She waddles across the kitchen, settles into a chair and props her feet up on another. No one says anything- we all watch in shocked silence as she polishes off the glass. "Love makes you do funny things, Nico. Would you ever have imagined Jason changing?"

"No," Austin answers for me.

"And you changed too, right?"

"Only because my life fell apart."

"But you changed. And you've found a way to forgive your brother."

"Working on it," I correct.

"So maybe Alison saw who you are, who you're becoming."

My stomach turns to lead. "I don't deserve her."

"Nope," Jason agrees. "But I don't deserve Millie either, and somehow she still loves me."

Millie beams across the table at him. "It's easy," she murmurs.

I turn to Danny. "Did you know about this?"

He shakes his head. "This is news to me. I met her dad about a year after they moved to Kansas City."

"You need to go find her, Nico," says Macey. "Talk to her. This doesn't have to be the end." She glances at Austin. I still haven't gotten their full story. Maybe some night over a bottle of scotch.

"You have to be prepared for her to tell you to fuck right off and go to hell, though," Jason adds. "'Cause that's what you deserve."

He's right. I deserve that and worse. I don't have the right to beg for mercy but I can't live with myself if I don't. I look over to my older brother, seeing him in an entirely new light. It took guts for him to come to us, it would have been easier for him to walk away, cut ties completely and move on without us. But he didn't- he took his lumps.

I think it will kill me if Alison tells me to go to hell. And if that's what she does, I'll spend the rest of my life atoning for it, and hope that maybe in the next life, I can do a better job of not fucking things up.

It's a shot in the dark, that she'll be at her house, but my calls are being directed to voicemail, and I don't know where else to try. I glance over at the bouquet of peonies and roses on the passenger seat. I'd buy her a carload if it will get her to talk to me. I've had hours to rehearse, to reflect. So many things make sense now- the initial tension when Alison first introduced me to her family. *They knew.* My gut clenches as the guilt roils my stomach for the umpteenth time.

I pull to a stop in front of the house, and a gust of relief blows through me when I see my rental car in the driveway. I drum the steering wheel, gathering my courage.

My thoughts return again to Jason. *Karma.* When does it end? I have to accept that it might not. I swallow down a lump. All I can do is try. I grab the bouquet and exit the car.

The door opens before I can knock, and Kimmie lets me have the full force of her wrath. "You think flowers are going to fix this?"

"I thought they could help."

She looks ready to slam the door in my face. "Let him in, Kimmie," her mother calls from inside. She glares at me but steps aside. Her parents are sitting on the couch, like they've been waiting for me.

I step inside and spy my favorite fuck-me-pink ankle boots as I begin to remove my shoes. Hope flares in my chest. "Mr. and Mrs. Park, let me start by saying how sorry I am. For everything. I had no idea-"

"You didn't. None at all," Kimmie interjects, and I can see my fight is going to be with her. She's the gate-keeper.

"Maybe some tea?" Mrs. Park offers.

"Mama, can't you see he doesn't deserve our hospitality?" Kimmie's voice rises.

Her mother stands. "Everyone deserves our hospitality."

"Please, I just want to talk to Alison."

Her father shakes his head. "I'm afraid that's not possible right now."

My heart jumps to my throat. "Why? Is she okay? Please, I just-"

"My sister is the strongest, most loving, kind-hearted, forgiving person I've ever known," Kimmie starts, voice shaking. "If it had been me, I'd have made you fall in love with me, then squashed you like a bug."

I have no doubt of that, and I have to respect the fierce love she has for her sister. "I didn't realize... I didn't know." My excuses are lame, and I'm sure to her they must seem empty. "When I was a teenager…" I clear my throat. "I was a horrible person. And I'm truly sorry I hurt your daughter-"

"It wasn't just Katie-bug," Kimmie interrupts. The nickname pierces my heart. "It was all of us."

"Enough, Kimberly," her father says. "This is Alison's story to tell."

"No, *abeoji*." She shakes her head vigorously. "It's our story too, he broke our hearts, too."

I'm filled with a sick kind of dread. "I don't understand."

"Let me spell it out. Your group tortured Katie to the point she was suicidal. I just happened to come home a day early from college to surprise everyone, and- and-" her voice catches, and she bats away a tear. "And she was in the bathroom with a handful of pills." She aims me a look so hateful that a shiver rolls down my spine. "An hour later, and she'd have been gone. She was smart, see? Too smart for her own good- she'd gone and researched the perfect toxic cocktail." She sniffs. "We nearly lost our brightest star because of you and your fucking friends and she *still* won't tell me what happened that day that pushed her over the edge."

I do. I take a step back, her words more painful than any of my brother's punches. My throat's so tight, I can't breathe. I wasn't lying when I told Alison I don't remember a ton about high school because I was stoned through most of it. But this, I do remember, clearly. Somehow, Lara had managed to steal her enormous underpants out of her gym locker, and she and our friend Pete had written 'fat ass' in black marker and strung them up the flagpole at lunch, while the rest of us stood around laughing. And I remember the next day, she wasn't in class. Or the day after that. She never came back.

The flowers slip from my hands as my knees buckle. I never wanted to die. As bad as it was with Jason, I never wanted to die. And I can't wrap my head around what the world would have missed out on, knowing who Alison/Katie is now.

"We got her help. And we moved back here, to Mama's hometown. And when Katie was better, she asked to change her name to her middle name. And I lost my sweet Katie-bug forever," Kimmie finishes. "So I appreciate your apologies, the flowers. But sorry doesn't cut it. Not for me. Never for me."

"That's enough now, Kimmie," her mother says.

I look at the three of them. Kimmie, standing arms crossed- judge, jury, and executioner- her parents looking torn apart. My eyes sting and I become hot all over. "I had no idea, and I swear, I will spend every day of the rest of my life making up for this. And if she'll have me, I will spend every day making sure Alison knows how loved she is- how much I love her." I think back to the words I exchanged with Jason. "I know my words may not have meaning right now, but if you'll give me the chance, I will show you. Every day."

Mrs. Park grabs a tissue and dabs at her eyes. Mr. Park speaks. "We love our daughter very much. And I believe you do to. And it is honorable for you to come here and offer your apologies. But Alison has been the one wronged, and it will be her choice who she lets into her life." His face turns to stone. "And we will fully support her in whatever decision she makes."

I nod, fully understanding his meaning, and sick with dread at the implications.

"But she is not here. She flew home to California this morning."

Of course. "I see."

Mr. Park raises a finger. "Kimberly is right about Alison. She is strong, and she has a gentle heart. Don't give up hope."

A gentle heart and a filthy mouth, I think wryly. And that's why I fucking love her.

Chapter Twenty-Nine

Alison

I'm exhausted. And covered in mud. I drop into the chair in my tiny office, and open my laptop. I've been home for three days, but I haven't had time to decompress and process the disastrous visit home. The first of the winter rains arrived in the form of an all-night gully washer. Carla and her crew and I have been repairing washed out fence posts, assessing exposed vines, and making a plan to get a cover crop planted as soon as possible to prevent further erosion this winter.

My heart hurts, reliving all the crap I thought I'd put behind me, all the self-loathing, that thankfully now feels foreign. I'm stronger now, I can see that clearly. And I have to admit, I'm stronger because of the way Nico loves me. He didn't tease me when I felt brave enough to let him see my affirmations on the bathroom mirror. He's never, not once, been repulsed by my curves, or my stretch marks. He sees the best version of me every day.

So why couldn't I tell him?

Shame. Pure and simple. There's no other reason. I'm ashamed of my former obesity, I'm ashamed that I was a victim- that I didn't have the skills to stop it, or the courage to tell someone who could. And Kimmie's been right this whole time. If I'm serious about letting him love me, he needs to know all of me- including the bits I'm ashamed of. I glance over at my phone, voicemail filled with his calls, none of which I've listened to. My hand hovers over the device, but then I hear a rumble and feel the earth shake. I clutch at the desk, momentarily filled with panic. Earthquake? Then I hear the distinctive whine of a semi. "Who ordered a delivery?" That truck sounds big and it's going to ruin the drive with all the mud.

I jog out of the office and raise the garage door. And shake my head to make sure I'm seeing what I think I'm seeing. For starters, there's an enormous moving van that's pulled up to the now-completed farmhouse. And Nico. Nico's leaning against the side of his car holding a box and an envelope. My heart leaps at the sight of him. He looks good. Yummy. He's in his James Bond suit, down to highly polished loafers that will be ruined in the mud if he takes even one step. I can't help but stare, because not only does my heart ache for him, my body does too.

He stares back, a hungry look in his eye. I cross the muddy expanse of yard and stop within arm's reach. "What are you doing here?"

He lifts the box. "You left your shoes at your parents."

My pink shoes. The ones that I still haven't wrapped around his neck. I let out a breathy laugh. "So I did."

His mouth kicks up and his eyes light in the triumphant way they do when he knows he's pulled one over on me. He extends the envelope.

"What's this?"

"I've been thinking."

"Just as long as it's not more wine names."

"Better. I got to thinking about our living situation, and how there's no room for an office for a wine conglomerate. And then I got to talking with Dec about your concern about who would own the property in the future."

For a hot second, my stomach drops to my toes. He's not here to talk, he's here to sack me. But he wouldn't look at me like he wanted to rip my clothes off, if he was through with me. Would he?

"So, I made a deal with Declan and Austin. I move headquarters here to Fieldstone, and Declan gives me the farmhouse."

I gasp, tears springing to my eyes. "Noooo. I was supposed to have right of first refusal. He promised." I glare at him, willing my tears to stay behind my eyelids. "It's in my contract, and I will sue your ass off for this. I swear, Nico."

He grins. "Open the envelope."

I grab it, and tear open the flap with shaking hands. I rifle through the papers, very quickly seeing it's the title to the winery, and my name's on every page. I shake my head. "I don't understand."

"Since you made it clear you won't live anywhere but here, and the trailer is too small for both of us *and* my office, I made a deal with Declan."

I can see where this is going, but I don't quite believe it yet.

"He agreed to be bought out only if you got the title. I made him a very generous offer on your behalf."

"But I don't have that kind of money."

His eyes light. "But I do."

"So now I owe you? There's no way I can pay you back. Not for years."

He shakes his head. "If it's so important to you to pay me back, I'm sure we can work out a plan that's…er…" his mouth quirks. "Mutually beneficial."

I study the paperwork again. "I really own this?"

"Mmmhmm. It says so right here, midway down the first page." He leans over and points to the first place my name shows up, arm brushing mine. My chest pounds as a hot current of want runs up my arm.

"I don't know what to say."

His voice is thick when he speaks. "Say you'll forgive me, or at least give me the chance to earn it every day for the rest of my life. I… have no excuse for the shitbag I was in high school, and I'm still struggling with the fact that you nearly ended things, and what my life would be like without you in it."

"You talked with my family."

"I did." He gently takes the papers, swings around and tucks them under the box which he places on the roof of the car. Then he turns back, takes my hands and drops to his knees. He starts by kissing the backs of them.

"You'll ruin your pants."

"Don't care." He tugs me down into the mud with him. Of course, I'm already covered, so I don't care either. "First things first- We've taken out restraining orders on Veronica and Lara, not only are they not allowed within five hundred feet of any of us, they're also banned from this property and any property connected with the Case family name."

I feel like a weight has been taken from me. One I didn't know I carried. I think I've spent most of my adult life looking over my shoulder, worried I might run into one of them.

He continues. "I behaved badly at the wedding. I should have-" but I stop his mouth with a kiss.

His arms wrap tightly around me and he deepens the kiss with a groan. I meet his tongue with a groan of my own. It's only been a few days, but I've missed him with an ache that's hard to describe. "I should have told you," I say when we break apart. "I was afraid you'd only see me the way I was, not the way I am now."

"I love *you*. The you that's in front of me."

"And I love you too- the best you, not the you who was a fucked-up teenager."

"I promise I'll spend the rest of my life making it up to you."

I shake my head. "You don't, I want us to be us, to not have the specter of the past hanging over us. There's something else I need to tell you, too."

"You're pregnant?"

He looks so hopeful, I burst into laughter. "No. And children are a conversation for another day." I shake my head. "No. I had lap band surgery about six months after my divorce."

He looks confused. "Why?"

"Because I was tired of the constant diets, of losing ten pounds and gaining five back. I... didn't like who I was, or how I felt. A-and I wanted a fresh start. That's part of why I don't eat much at one sitting."

His face is serious, when he speaks. "Do you like who you are now?"

"More since you've been in my life. It helps, hearing the constant verbal affirmation that I'm okay this shape. I'll never be... small." That's still something that eats at me, and maybe it always will, but I no longer look in the mirror and hate what I see, and that's a small victory.

"I don't care," he rumbles, kissing the spot on my neck that sends heat straight to my pussy. "I love you just the way you are right now, and whatever way you are in the future." He captures my mouth, kissing me with such tenderness tears spring to my eyes.

We'd still be kneeling in the mud kissing if not for the throat clearing of the truck driver. "Excuse me, Mr. Case? Do we have permission to unload?"

Nico turns to me. "I don't know, do we?"

"Have permission to move your headquarters into my farmhouse?"

He nods solemnly.

I can't help the grin that pulls my mouth up. "I, er, think we can reach a... mutually beneficial agreement."

Chapter Thirty

Nico

*I*t's bud-break. The winery is a riot of spring green- a new season, a new chapter of life. The perfect time for us to begin the newest chapter of our lives together. I've filled every corner of the crushing pad with bouquets and swags of pink peonies and roses, and about fifty of our closest friends and family stand with me as I wait for my future father-in-law to walk his breathtakingly beautiful daughter down the short aisle.

My brothers are here, all of them- Jason with Millie, and their daughter Sara Anne, Declan and Emmaline, and Austin, though Macey is home, about to bring another Case baby into the world.

I only have eyes for Alison, and she for me as she joins me up front. I take her hand and catch a flash of pink at her feet. I lean in and whisper. "Are those my favorite shoes?"

She side-eyes me with a smirk and an arch of her brow.

I fucking love this woman. She knows as soon as I can sneak her off to a corner what's happening. Those shoes have been wrapped around me plenty of times in the last few months, but this time will be sweeter, better. I'm so caught up in my fantasy I nearly miss the judge's question. "Do you Nico, take Alison to be your lawfully wedded wife, for better or worse, for richer or poorer, in sickness and in health, to love, forgive, and partner with in all things?" We added that last part, but we like it.

"Hell yes, I do," I say, leaning in to seal my promise with a kiss. I know it's not time to kiss her yet, but ask me if I care? Because of this woman, I've been given the most precious gift of a second chance- at life, at family, at love. And I'm not taking it for granted. Not for a second. So yeah- I'm kissing the bride. Twice. And as much as she'll let me until death do us part.

THE BEGINNING OF HAPPILY EVER AFTER

Thank you for reading. Nicholas & Alison's story. Are you ready for more bad boys?

Next, read about Danny & Roxi's forbidden workplace romance, fraught with secrets and suspense in MR. WHISKEY.

Mr. Whiskey is also the lead-in to my Titans of Tech Series- which you won't want to miss – a mix of Hero-Only POV and dual POV, this series is Naughty Rom-Com to the core!

For an Epic Alphahole takedown involving Forbidden Love, and an irresistible 4yo who helps bring Austin to his knees – Read MR. PINK!

For another Alphahole takedown involving secret identities, forbidden love, and a plot twist that will have you reaching for the Kleenex – read MR. WHITE.

Do you want to know more about Prairie? Meet Emmaline, Mason, and a whole host of hunky cowboys and sassy smart heroines in my alter-ego Tessa Layne's USA Today Bestselling series, The Cowboys of the Flint Hills.

HEART OF A COWBOY
family feud/fake engagement
HEART OF A REBEL
opposites attract/workplace
HEART OF A WRANGLER
second chance
HEART OF A HORSEMAN
star-crossed lovers/second chance
HEART OF A HERO
old flame/PTSD
HEART OF A BACHELOR
secret baby
HEART OF A BAD BOY
fake engagement
HEART OF A BULL RIDER
Doctor-patient/second chance
HEART OF A RANCHER
enemies to lovers

Do you love sneak peeks, book recommendations, and freebie notices? Sign up for my newsletter at www.tslayne.com!!

Find me on Facebook! Come on over to my house- join my ladies only Facebook group - Tessa's House. And hang on to your hat- we might get a little rowdy in there ;)

Meet the Roughstock Riders

A brand new steamy contemporary romance series filled with rodeo hotties and the women that bring them to their knees...

He's an ex-con. She's the sweet virgin he can never have.

When disgraced bull rider Ty Sloane agreed to take a job as foreman at Falcon Ridge Ranch, he didn't count on having to share his job or his cabin with twenty-one-year-old rising star barrel racer Maybelle Johnson. She tests his patience by day and drives him to distraction by night, but she's off limits—too young and innocent for the likes of an ex-con like him.

As far as Maybelle is concerned, Ty Sloane can go jump in a lake. The cocky bull rider is a thorn in her side, both at the ranch and on the road. But he makes her feel things no man has ever made her feel, and as she learns about his past, she can't help but develop a soft spot for him.

When trouble finds Maybelle on the rodeo circuit, Ty puts it all on the line for the sweet young woman who's captured his heart, even though it may cost him his freedom.

Download RIDE HARD today!

Also by TS Layne

TS Writes Bad Boys & Billionaires

MR. PINK

billionaire secret romance

MR. WHITE

billionaire secret identity

MR. RED

billionaire secret identity second chance

MR. WHISKEY

billionaire secret identity workplace

WILD THANG

billionaire secret crush sports romance

PU$$Y MAGNET

billionaire workplace sports romance

O MAGNET

billionaire fake engagement sports romance

BABY MAGNET

Did you know I have an alter-ego? Under the pen name Tessa Layne I write Alpha Cowboys & Hot Heroes

HEART OF A COWBOY

family feud/fake engagement

HEART OF A REBEL

opposites attract/workplace

HEART OF A WRANGLER

second chance

HEART OF A HORSEMAN

star-crossed lovers/second chance

HEART OF A HERO

old flame/PTSD

HEART OF A BACHELOR

secret baby

HEART OF A BAD BOY

fake engagement

HEART OF A BULL RIDER

Doctor-patient/second chance

HEART OF A RANCHER

enemies to lovers

———

A HERO'S HONOR

single parent/workplace

A HERO'S HEART

frenemies to lovers

A HERO'S HAVEN

secret identity

A HERO'S HOME

opposites attract

RIDE HARD

virgin/workplace/opposites attract

RIDE ROUGH

secret identity/frenemies to lovers

RIDE FAST

Acknowledgments

In so many ways, this book was deeply personal for me. Big confession here: I suffer- acutely- from body dysmorphia. It is crippling, and it doesn't matter what my weight is- I struggle to love my body the way it is- thinking- I'll be happy if I can just lose....

It's total bullshit of course... especially as women- our bodies change all the damn time. We get chubby in puberty, then slim up as we move into young womanhood. If we take birth control, our bodies may change again if we take birth control. They certainly change if you get pregnant, and breastfeed. And then it changes again in middle age, and finally menopause.. We **have** to learn to meet ourselves where we are. To love the person we see in the mirror- even if it's not the body that magazines, T.V., movies, the internet, or other people tell us we should have. I'm still working on all this too. It's a daily battle- to love my body... to love *me* just as I am. And if it is for you too- I wish you peace and light and love. I wish you a compassionate heart for yourself. You are beautiful and worthy- just as you are.

And then there are the themes of forgiveness running through the book. How does one find a way to forgive someone close to you that's hurt you? Nico figured it out with the help of Alison, but honestly? I'm still working on it.

There's one more book in this quartet- Danny Pendergast- honorary Case brother. He is bad to the bone and so, *so* sexy. And there's only one woman strong enough, badass enough to bring him to his knees- Roxi Rickoli. Stay tuned

As always- just like winemaking doesn't happen in a vacuum- neither does writing. I'm incredibly grateful for my team- Kara my editor, Chas the PR Wonderqueen, Erin my magic making assistant, my darling daughters, and my husband who has complete and total faith in me. And who tells me I'm cute. Every day.

Lastly- Thank *YOU* my readers. You have no idea how much your letters and reviews of support mean to me. How much your readership means to me. I feel incredibly fortunate to be able to bring you the stories of my heart. So as I wrap book number **15** (cue the confetti) I lift my glass to you!

xo

CPSIA information can be obtained
at www.ICGtesting.com
Printed in the USA
BVHW081552050321
601818BV00002B/481

9 781948 526111